Every story is a journey.

Enjoy the trip!

[signature]

FRIENDS IN HIGH PLACES

ROB SMALES

READ UNTIL YOU BLEED!

ROB SMALES

FRIENDS IN
HIGH PLACES

*For my son Thomas, who though already sixteen
still hugs me back, even in public
where it might be a little embarrassing.*

*From the time you were a child,
you've always been your own man,
and you have no idea
how proud that makes me.*

This book wouldn't be what it is if not for the aid of author and editor extraordinaire Stacey Longo. Stacey, you're the best writing/editing partner anyone could ask for, even when you highlight an entire page of my manuscript and the margin note is, "What the hell did I just read?"

It also wouldn't even be a book without Pete Kahle and Bloodshot Books. Pete, thanks for taking a chance on me.

CHAPTER 1

I THINK WE GOT AWAY CLEAN

Everything would've been different if we hadn't been such incredible assholes.

"Wait up, guys!"

"Aw, Christ." Jerry threw a glance over his shoulder. "It's Tagalong."

"Don't look back," I said. "Just walk faster. He'll give up—or his asthma will kick in."

Ignoring me, Ray slowed, looking back. "I say we flatten the little creep," he said, his hands already curled in tight fists.

Watching Ray beat up Tagalong wasn't my idea of a good time, but I also didn't want to get in Ray's way. Instead, I sped up and shouted back to him. "Remember the asthma? You'll probably kill him—besides, what if somebody sees you? What if a *grownup* sees you? You really want to be known as the guy who pounded Wheezy Taglioni? He's practically a cripple."

"Aw, shit." Ray dropped his fists and picked up his pace, pulling alongside of Jerry and me.

"Guys?" Now that I was listening for it, Tommy Taglioni's voice was a little breathy. "Guys, c'mon!"

"This is all your fault," Jerry said to Ray, who just shot him a look and said, "Ah, shut up and run for it," before suiting action to word and legging it down the street, tennis shoes slapping the sidewalk, wide jean cuffs flapping like a duck trying to take off. He hadn't gone a dozen steps before Jerry and I were running beside him; Ray might have been the biggest—and toughest—of us, but he was also the slowest. But even he was faster than Tommy Tagalong.

"Aw, guys, please... wait... up..."

It was already working. Short, fat, and wearing a pair of glasses with lenses as thick as my thumbs, Tagalong slowed as his trademark wheeze took over. We turned the corner from Tremont onto Fairview and I looked back and saw him standing there, big belly shaking as he sucked on the inhaler that usually rode around in his front pocket, making it look like he was really happy to see you. We ran a few more blocks before Ray dropped back to a walk. His chest was heaving, and maybe he didn't have to stop and put his hands on his knees, but he was wheezing nearly as badly as Tagalong himself.

"I think... the little bastard... quit and went home."

"Still your fault," said Jerry—then he danced back, easily avoiding Ray's fist. It had been a halfhearted swing; Ray was already out of breath, and besides, he knew Jerry was right.

We had walked to school all winter—thanks, mostly, to Ray leaving his bike in the driveway for his father to back the car over—through cold, snow, and ice, and in the spring, the trip, and hanging out with the guys first thing in the morning, was actually pretty cool... I mean, if you forgot about school being at the end of it. We never even thought of trying to beg a ride... at least, not until Mrs. Taglioni pulled up beside us in her brand new 1974 Buick LeSabre convertible. It was a thing of beauty, all decked out in showroom-shiny white walls and a chrome smile two yards wide, the rumble under the rich red hood enough to make the hair on the back of my neck stand up. It was May, and the morning had been warm, and she'd had the top down, the big lump of Wheezy grinning at us from the passenger's seat through his ever-present glasses.

"You boys need a ride?" she'd said, and before Jerry or I could say a word, Ray stepped forward and practically shouted, "Yes, ma'am!" Ray had always been a car guy, even when we were little and just pushing our Dinkys and Matchboxes around the kitchen floor. It was like the shiny new car had hypnotized him, and we'd just followed along as he climbed into the backseat, touching everything he could reach and gazing with longing at everything he couldn't.

That was the day Wheezy Taglioni decided he was going to be one of us. We'd stopped accepting rides from Wheezy's mom right away—even changed the route we took to school, so they couldn't accidentally meet with us again—but it was too late. The damage was done. After that, Wheezy's gasping little *wait up, guys* became a regular sound in our lives, like the class bells at school, or, once the seventh grade ended and summer vacation started, the jingling of the Mr. Softie truck.

Unlike Mr. Softie's bell, though, Wheezy's breathy little shouts always led to us running *away*, rather than toward him—and Wheezy would follow, chasing when we ran, and eventually showing up if he knew where we were going. That's how, in our minds at least, Wheezy Taglioni became Tommy Tagalong—though in his meaner moments, Ray called him Tommy Fagalong. It wasn't just that Jerry and Ray and I had grown up together, lived three in a row for as long as we could remember, and here came this kid who'd moved to the street just a couple of years earlier, a kid who couldn't run or play or anything, who thought he could just slip into our lives like he'd been here all along, but Tommy just wouldn't take no for an answer. The more we refused, the more he insisted—but the faster he followed, the farther we ran. Sometimes, lying in bed at night and thinking about stuff before I fell asleep, it would occur to me that he was kind of sad, and that as the new kid on the street we could also have called him Tommy Tagli-*lonely*. I never mentioned this to the guys, though; they would've called me a simp, or a wuss, and then left me behind to keep Tommy company for the day.

Just the thought made me shudder.

Ray was walking faster now, breathing easier, and I turned to walk backward a few yards, checking for signs of pursuit, like they did in those crime movies Mom doesn't like but Dad still watches with me. "I think we got away clean." I glanced at Ray. "You gonna be okay, old man?"

Ray, really the youngest of us even though he was the biggest, put up his dukes and danced closer, imitating that boxer Muhammad Ali, who he claimed was going to be the next heavyweight champ, though Jerry and I agreed there was no way the guy would beat Foreman. "Who you callin—" he started, but I spun to face front and walked even faster.

"You want to pick up the pace, then?"' I said. "We *do* want to get there today, right?" He settled down and the three of us started marching double time. We weren't trying to outrun Tagalong anymore, though: now we were just trying to cover the distance.

It was a two mile walk to the carnival.

CHAPTER 2

MOVE ALONG, KIDS; LET THE REAL CUSTOMERS THROUGH

It was late August, and August in Caina, Indiana, meant carnival. The name on the side of the trucks as they drove through town was DINGALING BROS FAMILY CIRCUS AND SIDESHOW, and that was what the big sign above the entry gate said, but we just called it the carnival. After a whole summer of doing nothing—because that was what there was to *do* in Caina, Indiana—watching those big, colorful trucks make their way along Main Street toward the edge of town was like that part of the movie where some flunky runs in with a pardon from the governor. Suddenly we all knew just how the guy trussed into Old Sparky felt when they unbuckled the straps without turning him extra-crispy: like we'd been holding our breath for months, and right then it came out all at once, *whoosh*, and we could breathe again.

Our T-shirts stuck to our backs as the big gate with its ticket booth came into view, and though August meant school was right around the corner, for the moment I was happy it wasn't still July: the walk would have been a lot more miserable. We hustled along, a little out of breath in the heat, and as we approached the gate I stuck my fingers into the front pocket of my jeans, feeling for the wad of singles I'd stuffed in there. I'd managed to save a little more than eighty dollars over the summer, working in my uncle's shop, but the carnival was here for ten days; if I rationed myself to twenty bucks a trip, I could make at least four trips, and—

"Hi, guys!"

I stopped so fast Jerry walked right into me, and Ray whispered a quick "Son of a bitch!" Beside the gate, sunlight glinting off his Coke-bottle glasses and sweat rings under his arms the size of truck tires even though he was standing still, was Tagalong. He waved toward the parking lot, and from a red convertible sitting along its edge, his mom waved back. As she drove away, top down, the kerchief tied over her hair fluttering in the wind, we all looked back at Tommy, and it occurred to me that, beautiful machine or not, I really hated that car.

"You guys almost forgot me," he said as we trudged up to the ticket booth. "Good thing my mom gave me a ride. She can give us a ride home, later, too." Ray and Jerry just walked by him without a glance, paid their five bucks, and took their tickets. While I waited my turn at the window, I considered what Tommy had just said. He'd shouted to us, and we'd looked right at him and then run. There was no way he hadn't seen that. But here he was, saying we'd just forgotten him, acting like it had all been a big mistake, like if he claimed it loud enough it would somehow become what had actually happened. The name *Tommy Tagli-lonely* wormed its way through my head, and I couldn't help it: I flashed him a quick, guilty smile.

I turned away, hoping he hadn't seen, stepping up to the window for my ticket. But whether he'd seen or not didn't really matter: he'd already bought his own ticket, so when the three of us walked into the carnival, it was with Tommy Tagalong yapping at our heels like the world's most asthmatic puppy.

Four hours later, he wasn't yapping: he was whining. "C'mon, guys! I'm tired. Can't we just go wait for my mom? Please? *Please?*"

The whining had actually started in the first hour and grown steadily worse as the day went on. At the roller coaster (*Oh, that doesn't look safe!*). At the Zipper (*My God, those things spin?*). Even at Dr. Terror's Ten-In-One, where there was a snake man, a bearded lady, and—coolest of all—the preserved body of a two-headed wolf in a huge glass jar, he complained about the smell coming from the pickled punks—complained so loud the barker in the old-fashioned white shirt and straw boater told us to "Move along, kids; let the real customers through."

It occurred to me that for someone who wanted to do everything we did, Tagalong didn't really want to *do* anything. He didn't even go on the roller coaster, or the Zipper, or the Tilt-A-Whirl, or anything else we tried, but waited in line with us at each ride or attraction and was right there when we got off, whining loudly the whole time. The only thing he wanted to ride was the carousel—but he wouldn't go alone and begged us to go with him.

"I wouldn't go on that merry-go-round with him for a thousand bucks," said Ray as we settled in to ride the Turkish Twist.

"Not for a million," said Jerry.

"What are we gonna do?" I said, and we all looked out at the people still lined up for the ride. Right in the front, a squat, toadlike shape flapped a hand, shouting "Guys? I don't think this is a good idea!"

"We have to think of something," said Jerry, and then the warning horn sounded, the ride shuddered into motion, and for the next four minutes all I heard were screams of excitement as the carnival spun around us in a blur.

"Good thing he held out 'til the ride was over." Ray hooked a thumb toward Deano Gordon, a kid a year younger than us who was noisily depositing his guts into the trash barrel by the Twist's exit ramp. "Woulda been messy as hell if he puked on the—"

"See?" Tagalong bustled out of the crowd like someone's indignant grandmother, pointing a finger toward Deano while obviously trying not to look at him. "I knew this wasn't a good idea! Why don't you guys ever listen? I try to—"

"Come on," said Jerry, shouldering past Tommy and looking back at us. "I have an idea." Ray's fists were bunched again, and he stared at Tagalong, who half turned after Jerry to shout, "I'm only trying to help!" I nudged Ray's elbow to get his attention and jerked a chin toward Jerry's disappearing back. We brushed past Tommy, heard him squeal in surprise, and started to hustle. We followed Jerry as he slid through the popcorn-and-cotton-candy-scented crowd the way only a smaller kid can, past the sharpshooting booth (ten shots for two bits!) and the ring toss (a winner every time!) and found him already in line for a new ride.

"The Ferris wheel?" I said. "That's your idea?"

"Only costs a half a buck," Jerry said with a smile. "And it's the longest ride at the carnival."

"That's because it's the slowest," said Ray—and suddenly I thought I understood.

"Sometimes a Ferris wheel ride can take ten minutes," I said. "Maybe more."

"But that—" Ray started.

"That's ten minutes without Tagalong," said Jerry. "Maybe more."

Ray's frown continued. "What are you—"

"You guys... shouldn't run... off like that." Tommy pushed his way through the crowd with one hand, the other hovering at his hip like one of those old-time gunfighters in the westerns, ready to quick-draw his inhaler in case he needed to take a nice quick suck. At the sound of his wheezing little voice, Ray's frown faded away, leaving him grinning like one of those *Have a Nice Day* pins you could buy at the corner store.

"You're a genius!"

"Yeah, I know." Jerry buffed his nails against his chest. "I'm just glad you finally—"

He broke off, staring past us. I turned to look and saw only Tagalong, finger still raised to scold but mouth blissfully silent, staring up at the Ferris wheel, an odd look in his lens-magnified eyes. I glanced back to Jerry and saw the line had moved ahead, but we hadn't moved with it.

"Hey." I pointed toward the entry ramp. "Do we want to ride this thing today, or what?"

"What?" said Jerry. "Yeah, I... yeah." He faced front and stared at the wheel, ignoring me and Ray just as we ignored Tagalong's "Guys? I don't think this is a good idea."

Jerry stayed quiet while we were in line, and when our turn came he managed to finagle himself a solo ride while I shared a car with Ray. Ray, despite what he'd said about the wheel being the slowest ride, had himself a ball, whooping like a madman, ignoring the instructions we'd gotten from the ride attendant and setting the car to rocking, shading his eyes with one hand sometimes and shouting, "I can see my house from here!" Whenever the wheel lined up right, and I could see Jerry, he was sitting in his car quietly, staring toward the ground. I wondered what was eating him, but figured I'd hear about it soon enough: Jerry's not exactly the tightest-lipped guy you ever met. I was right: it only took until we all met up by the wheel's exit ramp.

"Guys, I have an idea."

"Another one?" I said.

"Is it as good as the last one?" Ray said.

"Shut up and listen. Did you see Tagalong's face when he looked at the Ferris wheel?"

"He tells us to shut up," said Ray. "Then he asks us a question?"

"He looked a little weird," I said, ignoring Ray. "But he always looks weird."

"He didn't just look weird," said Jerry. "He looked terri—oh, crap, here he comes. Just follow my lead, okay?"

Ray looked baffled, and I was confused, but we nodded just as Tommy wheezed to a stop beside us.

"Rocking the car like that was dangerous," he said to the side of Ray's head; Ray just stared hard at me. "What were you thinking? I mean, do you know—"

"Hey, Wheez—I mean, Tommy," interrupted Jerry. "We give you kind of a hard time, huh?"

There were a few beats of silence as Tagalong stared at Jerry, his normally smooth red cheeks going blotchy; when his answer came it was much quieter than when he'd been dressing down Ray. "Yeah."

"We take off on you, make you chase us, call you Tagalong, all that stuff, right?"

Tommy looked at the ground, and murmured, "Yeah."

"How would you like to just hang with us, no more having to chase us or anything, you know, as one of the gang?

Tommy looked up, his face brightening. "Yeah?"

"Yeah," Jerry said.

"Yeah!"

Ray and I stared at each other, and Ray's eyes looked as wide as mine felt. What the hell was this?

"Okay," said Jerry, and Tommy Taglioni straightened, grinned, and did a weird sort of whole-body wiggle like an excited puppy. I eyeballed the front of his jeans to see if he'd wet his pants.

"But!" Jerry said, loud and clear, cutting through Tagalong's excitement. Tagalong went still. "You have to do something first. To prove you're one of us." He half turned to indicate me, and Ray, and then himself, sketching a kind of triangle in the air, and with the eye Tagalong couldn't see he threw us a big wink, like they do on TV.

"That's right," I said.

"We all had to do it," said Jerry.

"We did?" said Ray. I poked an elbow into his ribs. "*Oof.* I mean, we did. Yes, we sure did."

"The thing is," Jerry went on, "you don't get to pick what you do. We do. And if you don't do it, then you're not one of us, and you don't get to be part of the gang. No more following along, or chasing us down, you dig? It's like an initiation, and if you don't make it, you're out."

Tagalong stared at him.

"You dig?" Jerry said again.

Tommy swallowed and nodded, fingering the outline of the inhaler in his pocket like some kind of good luck charm. "What do I have to do?"

Jerry threw a thumb over his shoulder. "All you gotta do is ride the wheel."

The blood ran out of Tommy's face like someone had pulled the plug in his neck. "Oh, I don't think—"

"At night," said Jerry.

"But I—"

"After they close," Jerry added. "In the dark."

Tommy's eyes shut and he licked his lips, squeezing the shape of that inhaler so hard his knuckles went all white. "I'm..." He took a raspy breath. "I'm... afraid of heights."

"Uh-huh." Jerry didn't sound surprised at all. "Well, then," he went on, his voice loud and jolly, like some of the better barkers on the midway. "Good thing you'll be doing it at night, huh? You won't be able to see how high up you are, what with the dark and all." He grinned. "So, are you in? Or are you ready to admit you're just not one of us and go home?"

I held my breath. Beside me, I don't think Ray was breathing either. Tommy Taglioni opened his eyes and looked up, then higher, leaning his round head back on his fat little neck as he took in the whole Ferris wheel. We were standing practically at the base of the ride, and his chin didn't stop rising 'til he was looking almost straight up. My lungs burned, pushing me to take a breath, but I didn't want to do anything to break the moment, to make a sound that might interfere with Tommy's—

"I'm in." The words were barely above a whisper. Air whooshed out of me, and I heard Ray take a big, whooping breath.

"What?" Jerry leaned in, cupping an ear. "I couldn't quite hear you."

Tommy dropped his gaze to Jerry. "I'm... I'm in." His wheeze was creeping back in, almost as loud as his words. "I'll do it. When?"

"Tonight," Jerry said. "The carnival closes at ten. We'll do it at midnight."

"Where do we—"

"Here. Meet us right here at the wheel. At midnight." He looked at me and Ray. "You guys agree?"

I looked at Ray, who shrugged and nodded, so I gave Jerry a "Yeah, sure."

Tommy swallowed. His breathing was getting worse. "How do I—"

"Up to you," said Jerry. "Getting here is part of the challenge." He pointed to the ground at his feet. "But we'll be right here at midnight. Waiting." He started walking away, waving for me and Ray to follow. "We're gonna take off now. You wait here for your mom—and don't say anything about this to her, or any grownup, or you forfeit. The next time we see you will be here, at midnight."

We left him staring up at the Ferris wheel, eyes huge behind those Coke-bottle lenses. Before we'd gone a half-dozen steps I heard the sharp hiss of his inhaler as Wheezy Taglioni gave himself a blast.

"It's perfect!" Even in the heat, Jerry was practically dancing, spinning around to face us, walking backward as we put some distance between us and the carnival gate, where Tagalong would soon be waiting for his mom. Jerry had ignored our questions, including Ray asking, "What the hell's going on?" again and again, and herded us toward home with a smile on his face, but he couldn't hold it in any longer. Like I said: not exactly the tightest-lipped guy.

"I'm gonna perfectly bruise your ass, you don't tell us what's going on," said Ray, frustration in his voice.

Jerry grinned wider. "Pervert!"

"That's not what I—"

"Just tell us what's going on," I said. "Before the pervert really does bruise your ass."

"Hey!"

"It's perfect," Jerry repeated, then he lost the grin for a minute. "Wait—you guys can sneak out tonight, right?"

"Unless I get caught," I said. Ray just nodded.

"Good. So, tonight we get rid of Tommy Tagalong once and for all."

"How?" I said.

"You heard the whole thing already. We go to the carnival tonight, and by morning, no more Tagalong!"

"I don't get it," said Ray. I thought I knew what Jerry was getting at, but it still didn't make a lot of sense.

"Tagalong agreed to leave us alone if he fails, right?" said Jerry. "So how do you think he's gonna get in to meet us?"

"Climb the fence," said Ray. "I mean, that fence is a joke. If they didn't have people watching for—"

"It's a joke for us," I pointed out. "But this is Wheezy. Jerry's right: that might stop him right there." I looked at Jerry. "But what if it doesn't? What if the little turd makes it in? What then?"

"Then we offer him a ride."

We stared at him. He slowed to a halt, and so did we, standing there eyeballing him in the late summer sun.

"Look, you saw his face at the wheel: he was terrified just looking at that thing. There's no way he's got the sack to actually go on it. I saw the chain they use to lock up the lever at night, and it's just got a padlock—you can crack that, right?"

I'd made that money for the carnival working at my uncle's shop: my uncle's *locksmith* shop. He'd given me some tools and shown me the basics, and I'd had all summer to practice; unless it was something pretty expensive and high tech, I was pretty sure I could open a padlock. I nodded.

"So that's it. We open the panel while he's standing there looking at the thing—give him some time to take a good, long gander—then ask him to take a seat. When he doesn't, it's bye-bye Tagalong!"

"What if he does?" I said. "You said if he goes for the ride then we'll hang with him all the time. So what if he does?"

"Yeah," said Ray. "What if he does? I'm not hanging with Fagalong. No way. *You* said it, *you* do it."

Jerry shrugged. "If he wants a ride, then we give him one. I watched the guy running it, and it looks simple enough. We can even run the wheel without the lights, so no one will see it in the dark—but they'll hear the motor. So, we give Tagalong his ride and then run for it. The carnies come out to see about the racket, and Tagalong can't run worth a damn, so he gets caught."

"But if he goes for the ride," I said, "we have to hang with—"

"Do you really think if Tagalong gets caught he'll be able to keep his mouth shut?"

"So, we have to hang out with him *and* we get in trouble?" I was amazed—and not in a good way. "What the hell kind of a plan is—"

"And do you really think," Jerry went on, unruffled, "that if we get her baby boy in that much trouble—and they'll probably call the cops—Mrs. Taglioni will ever let Tommy see us again? I mean, ever?"

"I—" I began, but stopped as my brain rolled his plan over again. For once, Ray seemed to be ahead of me.

"So," he said. "If he doesn't go for the ride, he can't hang with us anymore. And if he does go for the ride... he can't hang with us anymore." He stepped forward and clapped Jerry on the shoulder, and his grin was absolutely huge. "You're a genius!"

Jerry shrugged, smiling right back. "Yeah, I know."

"We'll get some heat if he takes the ride," I said.

"Worth it," Ray said. "So worth it."

"If it'd be too much heat for you," Jerry said, "you could stay home. Maybe we can find some other way to unlock the lever."

He sounded serious, but I knew what they'd think if I didn't go: *pussy*.

"So," I said. "We'll meet at the end of the street around eleven?"

Jerry shook his head. "Baker Street," he said, naming the next road over from ours. "Don't want to take a chance on running into Tagalong on his way there and wind up listening to him wheeze and whine for two miles."

"It's a plan!" Ray announced. We spent the rest of the walk home in deep discussion, laughing about what we thought would happen that night at the Ferris wheel that stretched into the sky, visible above trees and houses long after the rest of the carnival had disappeared from view.

We had no idea.

CHAPTER 3

OR GET OFF THE POT

"**W**hat time is it?"

"Sixty seconds later than the last time you asked me," I told Jerry. "Will you just relax?"

It was ten before midnight, and we'd already been there ten minutes, lurking in the shadows beside the big, skeletal wheel. We'd gotten there early, urged on by a thought I'd had while sneaking out of the house: What if we got there and found Tagalong trying to get over the fence? He'd start begging us to help him for sure. *But*, I'd said, *if we got there first...*

So, we'd hustled along—the night was much cooler than the day—gone over the temporary fence without any trouble, and I'd spent the rest of the time answering the same question every minute or so. We'd been really looking forward to it while making our plans that afternoon, but it turned out being in the carnival at night was actually spooky as hell: without all the people, lights, and noise, it was a silent place filled with weird shapes that threw even weirder shadows. We were hiding in the deep shadows—but if we could do it, others could too, and my imagination populated the dark places around us with all kinds of things, angry carnies the least of them. I complained about the guys asking the time, but I was actually glad for the distraction; the only other thing I had to do was to look about for things that might be looking at *us*.

"What time is it?" said Ray—apparently another minute had passed.

"It's—"

"Hi guys," said the deep darkness right beside Ray.

"Shit!" Ray half shouted, lunging away from the voice.

"Jesus," whispered Jerry, and I forced my heart down out of my throat as one shadow broke off from the rest and stepped toward us; a short, fat shadow, with an inhaler in one hand.

Ray came around fast, fist up and ready to punch. "You think that's funny?" he said through gritted teeth, volume rising.

I stepped between them as Tagalong scrambled back, round lenses catching a bit of moonlight, holding up his inhaler like some sort of shield. "Easy, Ray," I said, then stepped close to whisper: "You go waking people up now, too early, and it'll be a push. You want all this to be for nothing?"

He glared at me for a second like I was the enemy, then jerked his head away and let out a pent-up breath. "Fine," he said as he turned and stomped toward the wheel's control panel.

I turned to Tommy, slowly releasing a held breath of my own and suppressing a grin. Now that it was over, I had to admit it had been pretty funny, the way the little feeb had snuck up on us. It had almost gotten him pounded flat, but it was still funny. "You ready?"

"Why did he—"

"You ready?" I repeated, cutting off the whine before it gained any speed and pointing up at the looming wheel. He turned, his head tilting back as he took it all in again, just like he had that afternoon. This time, though, the moon and darkness painted him in black and white, his glasses catching the weak light again and turning his eyes into flat, silver discs. Standing statue-still like that, he reminded me of some character from the funny pages—but from his expression, he was a long way from having fun. The only thing moving in this little scene was the shadow under his chin, pulsing, though the chin itself was still. I realized that beneath the roll of fat he wore like a collar, his Adam's apple was going up and down like a toe keeping a fast beat.

"Well," I said. "Ready or not..." I walked to the locked control lever where Jerry waited, penlight in hand.

"How did he get here?" he whispered.

I shrugged. "Search me. Asked his mom for a ride? Try to hold it steady, all right?"

He nodded, cupping a hand around the end of the torch, and his fingers glowed slightly when he turned it on. He parted two fingers, allowing a thin spear of light to hit the padlock while trapping the rest in his loose fist.

"That's good," I said, digging the tools Uncle Danny had given me out of my pocket and kneeling to work. It took almost five minutes for me to pop the lock—the hasp was tight, and the old Yale was down at a weird angle to work in—and I kept peeking over my shoulder to check on Tommy; as far as I could tell, he never moved.

"There we go," I whispered, finally pulling the padlock loose.

"Awesome," murmured Jerry. "I was watching the guy while we were in line. Forward spins it one way, backward the other, and the center is dead stop. The hand-grip is either a brake or a clutch. I'll figure it out enough for one ride. I think that switch works the lights and music. All we really need is power."

"There's gas in this thing," Ray said from the motor at the base of the wheel. "We should be good to go. But it's gonna be loud."

"Yeah, I know." Jerry shrugged. "We'll have to be quick, like I said." He looked past me, then jerked his chin in Tagalong's direction. "You think you can...?"

I nodded and went to Tommy, still silently staring up at his own four-story nightmare. His fingers had joined his jumping Adam's apple, rhythmically squeezing his inhaler in time with his working throat.

"It's now or never, Tagalong."

Tommy just gazed up at the wheel. I gave him a few seconds, wondering if he even heard me; he was staring pretty hard. It was getting spooky. I glanced at Jerry and Ray. They shrugged. *Great,* I thought. *Lot of help there.* Trying to snap him out of it, I wound up and gave Tagalong a hearty slap on the back and hit him with one of my dad's favorite sayings: "Come on, kid, it's time to shit or get off the pot."

Tommy staggered a bit and his chin snapped down, throwing his glasses to the end of his nose, revealing his unmagnified, piggy little eyes.

He looked up at me and for a second, I thought he would burst into tears. Then he turned without a word, and I put it down to the darkness and the odd sight of those naked eyes, usually hidden behind Tagalong's specs. He waddled over to the gate through the small fence around the wheel: there was just a chain running from pole to pole for the operator to unhook and let kids in two or three at a time. Ray had stepped over it on his way in to the motor, but little Tommy squatted to slip under, like a boxer entering the ring.

"Enjoy your ride," said Jerry, then added an evil "Muhahahaha!" It was corny and overdone, but Tagalong froze beneath the chain, and I heard him swallow. Behind him Jerry grinned, his teeth gray in the dim. I didn't grin back. I might have hated Tagalong's almost constant whining, but his silence now was making me nervous, and I just wanted to get this over with. I gave him a poke in the rump that made him start with surprise.

"Or get off the pot," I said.

He shuffled awkwardly through, then I stooped and followed. One of the cars was lined up with the loading platform, and it only took a moment to figure out the latch for the safety bar. "Take a seat," I said, swinging the bar wide. He started forward but stumbled as he passed me. I caught his arm and kept him from rolling ass-over-teakettle into the car—and that arm was vibrating like a plucked guitar string.

It was no wonder he was so quiet: the kid was frigging terrified.

Terrified, but still moving onto that Ferris wheel gondola on his own; no one was dragging him, he was making himself get on that ride. I wondered for a moment if I could've gone through with *anything* that made me that afraid, and I had to admit I didn't like the answer. Then Tommy Taglioni was centered in the seat, as far as he could get from either side, his hands pressing down on his lap like he was trying to pin himself to the earth with that inhaler. I pushed the safety bar into the latching system with a click, rather than the loud clatter the operator had made that afternoon.

The carny's spiel came back to me, and I repeated it to Tommy, loud enough so the guys could hear: "Keep your hands inside the car at all times, do not rock the car, and when the ride comes to a stop, please remain in your seat until I come let you out." Then, giving the bar a little shake to make sure it was latched, I whispered, "You can do this. Just hold on, and it'll all be over. You'll be fine."

He didn't say anything, just sat there, wheezing slightly, shoving his fists against his lap and staring at me, his face a fat, expressionless mask. I stepped back and whirled a finger in the air, like some western movie trail boss telling his crew to mount up, and said "Make it quick, guys."

The engine coughed, died, coughed again, and died. Ray swore and wound up to really yank the cord a third time. The machine coughed, sputtered, then finally caught, and the burbling roar of the Ferris wheel engine filled the night.

"Here we go," Jerry shouted—no need for silence now—as he squeezed the handle and eased the lever forward. The wheel lurched into motion, the car swinging up away from the platform. A strangled scream came from Tagalong, and as the car rose into the air I saw he was no longer trying to hold himself down out of the sky: both hands clutched the safety bar like a lifeline.

Just hang on, Tommy, I thought. Being caught by the carnies and cops would be bad for the kid, I knew, but from the look on his face when he'd been standing there, I was pretty sure the worst part of his night was happening right now. We were going to have to run soon if we didn't want to get caught ourselves, so all Tommy had to do was get over the hump and back down to the ground, and we'd—

The roar of the motor suddenly died. The wheel slowed, then shuddered to a stop, Tommy's gondola just one spot from the top, rocking slightly in the breeze. My startled gaze shot to the control lever, where Ray already stood by Jerry. He saw me looking and waved an arm in a whole-body *come hither, asshole!*

"Come on!"

I glanced up at Tommy's gondola, nearly four stories from the ground, and heard again his halting admission from that afternoon: *I'm... I'm... afraid of heights.*

"What happened?" I shouted hoarsely, reflexively still trying to be quiet.

"Come on!" Ray yelled again. "You wanna get caught?"

No, actually, I did not want to get caught. I looked up again. Tommy was trapped, with no way to get to the ground, but... I looked across the empty carnival. Jerry and Ray were no longer waiting but sprinting past the Hall of Mirrors and disappearing into the shadows. From where I stood, I could see where the carny folk had set their trailers and campers; lights were flickering on, and more than one shout rang through the night.

Crap.

"Sorry, Wheezy!" I vaulted the wheel's low fence and sped off after my friends. They had a heck of a head start, but Jerry must have been holding back to run with Ray, because I caught up with them at the fence by the customer parking lot; Ray was just going over the top, while Jerry looked back at me from the other side.

"What happened?" I shouted.

"Just climb!" Jerry shouted back, but I had already hit the fence running. I practically flew over it with all the fear and adrenaline in my system, and Ray and I hit the ground on the other side at the same time. He stumbled, out of breath, and I hooked my arm under his to yank him up: in my imagination, every carny in the world was riding down on us like the Indians rolling over Custer, and Ray could damn well catch his breath when we were safe at home. Ray got his feet under him and I started to run—but

Ray caught the arm I'd propped him with and yanked me back like a dog who'd run out the length of his lead.

"What are you doing?" I shouted. "We have to go. Tagalong'll tell 'em which way we went, and then they'll be aft—"

"He won't tell them anything for a while," said Jerry.

"What are you talking about?"

Jerry just pointed to Ray, who, still bent over with a hand on one knee, held something up for me to see: a little black T with a bit of rope dangling from the bottom. I stared.

"Is that the..."

Jerry nodded. "The starter pull-rope handle for the Ferris wheel's engine. Gonna be a while before they get Wheezy down and he can tell 'em anything."

I had a sudden flash of Tommy's white-knuckled fingers rising up and out of sight, holding tight to the gondola security bar, and remembered thinking that he was getting on that gondola even though it terrified him. What would happen, I wondered, when he found out the nightmare ride wasn't ending quickly? That it might go on for hours—at least until they figured a way to get him down from the now-frozen wheel.

"What happened?" I said, but Jerry just shrugged. I looked down at Ray, trying to sound cool, though my stomach churned. "You pull too hard? Don't know your own strength?"

"Cut it," said Ray, finally straightening. "Right before I shut the motor down."

I looked at Jerry, who shrugged again, then back to Ray. "What the hell was that ab—"

"He scared me," said Ray, and he sounded angry. "He came out of the dark like that and you guys heard me. Fat little faggot thought it was funny."

I'd seen the kid's face and he hadn't thought it was funny, hadn't thought *anything* was funny. I was about to say that, actually, *I'd* been the one who'd found it amusing, but Ray took a half-step toward me and, though he didn't raise a fist, they were clenched again. "Well, who's laughing now, huh? Ha! Ha-ha!"

Ray really was angry, and part of the reason, I realized, the reason he was looming over me a bit, was that he was angry with me for making him admit he'd been scared, when I could have been like Jerry and just gone along with it.

"Okay, okay." I raised my hands. "You've had your revenge, big guy—I saw the kid getting on, remember? He about crapped his pants just sitting in the seat. I don't think we'll even have to wait for Mrs. Taglioni to tell him to stay away from us. I think he'll do that on his own."

Jerry laughed, and even Ray chuckled. He was still chuckling when he started for home, swinging that handle around on its short cord like a cowboy doing rope tricks. Jerry turned to follow, but I hung back, studying the huge shape of the wheel, dark without its festive lights, standing there looking down on everything around it.

"You think he'll be okay up there?"

"You worried he's gonna be lonely?" said Ray over a shoulder.

"No. He was scared spitless, and I'm wondering what that'll do to his asthma—especially now that he's not coming down any time soon."

Ray spun to face me, but Jerry slipped smoothly between us. "Kid has his inhaler. You saw it—it wasn't even in his pocket, he was so ready to use it. He was probably sucking on the thing before the wheel even stopped. He'll be fine."

I nodded, recalling how he'd raised the inhaler against Ray like a talisman, then stumbled onto the gondola squeezing it 'til his knuckles turned white. There was something wrong here, something I couldn't put my finger on, but Jerry was right: Tommy had his inhaler, and he was ready to use it. He might be scared, but he should be fine. I nodded again. "We're going to catch so much heat for this when they get Wheezy down."

"Totally worth it," said Ray, turning toward home again.

CHAPTER 4

WHAT'S GOING ON
ACROSS THE STREET?

The racket dragged me out of a sound sleep. My eyes popped open, and I lay there a minute, watching my bedside clock: 6:03 flipped over to 6:04, a change I hadn't actually seen (at least, not the a.m. version) since school had let out for the summer. Now that I was awake I heard the shower running upstairs as Dad got ready to go to work, and Mom out in the kitchen making his breakfast and lunch, but all the noise from the street was what had woken me. I kicked loose from the tangled sheet that was my only blanket in the summertime and shuffled blearily down the hall into the living room. The side windows were open, creating (according to my pop) a cross breeze, and thanks to them I'd clearly heard engines shutting down and car doors slamming—but it was through the big plate window facing the street that I actually saw them.

Three police cars parked right in front of the Taglioni house.

I suddenly felt that cross breeze my dad was always hoping for, but not on my skin; I felt it on the inside, like someone had opened a pair of doors on me, front and back, and turned my belly into a breezeway, all airy and hollow and cool.

Jeeze, I thought. *They did call the cops! Like, all the cops! Is this because Ray broke the motor?*

"What's going on over there?"

I belted out a little "Eeep!" and I think my feet left the floor, but it was just my mom coming in behind me, curious about the racket herself.

"I dunno what's going on over there," I said, the words falling all over themselves trying to get out of me. "How should I know what's going on over there? That's over there and I'm over here. I dunno. How should I know?"

"Jeeze Louise, calm down," she said, peeking out the window. "No wonder you sleep so late all the time—you're a wreck when you get up this early."

"Hey, Julie?" yelled my dad, and I realized the shower upstairs had stopped. "What's going on across the street?"

"I have it on good authority that we don't know," she called back, shooting me a sideways smile. "But I'm sure we'll find out. Don't worry, I'll call you at the office if we don't hear 'til later. Promise."

The phone rang on its little table beside the couch. I picked up the handset, eyes still on the house across the street where Mrs. Taglioni was just opening the door.

"Hello?"

"Can you see what's going on?" Jerry didn't sound panicked, but more like he wanted to be, the words no louder than normal, but coming really fast. "I can't see too good from here. You got a better angle. Can you see what's going on?"

Jerry lived next door to us, and Ray was on our other side. We lived in the middle, right across the street from the Taglionis, and when they opened their front door you could usually see straight inside. This morning, though—

"There's too many cops, I can't see," I said, quietly trying out Jerry's normal-tone-fast-talking technique. "Tommy's mom opened the door, but I couldn't—"

"The cops come to talk to you," he said in a hurried stage whisper, "you were asleep and don't know nothing. Remember that: you don't know nothing."

"I don't—" I started to repeat, but a sharp click let me know Jerry was gone. A little shaken, I put the handset back in the cradle—and the phone rang while it was still in my hand, scaring the hell out of me. I snatched it back up.

"Hello?"

"Can you see what's going on?" Ray *did* sound panicked.

"No. Like I just told Jerry—"

A scream split the air, arrowing across the street and through the open windows to fill our little living room.

"My God!" shouted my mother as the scream came again.

"Gotta go," I said into the phone. "Something's happening!"

But I wasn't telling Ray anything he didn't know; the line was already dead.

"We're not making any accusations, sir. We're canvassing the neighborhood, talking to people who knew Tommy Taglioni, trying to find out if anyone heard or saw anything that can point us in the right direction."

My father stared at the officers standing just inside our front door, a whip-thin wall in shirtsleeves and tie who'd placed himself directly between me and the cops. "Is that right?"

"Yes, sir. Sometimes people know stuff they don't think is important. It could possibly help the investigation."

My father continued to stare.

The other cop, younger and impatient looking, finally sighed. "Look, buddy, we're just trying to find out what happened to the boy across the street. For his *mom*."

One of my dad's shoulders twitched at that, like they'd given him a sharp little shove. "Fine. But he doesn't know anything." He stepped back and aside—though still between the cops and the couch, where me and Mom sat—and gave me a tight little *be my guest* sweep of the arm. "Go ahead, tell them you don't know anything."

I looked at the cops, my eyes hot, but dry: I didn't know if crying would look guilty or just sad, and the confusion helped keep the tears away. My voice was still choked when I said, "What happened to Tommy?"

The first cop, the older one, stepped up even with my father without actually crossing Dad's invisible line, and knelt, putting his eyes more on a level with mine. "That's what we're trying to find out, son. All I know is that his mother says he went to bed as usual last night, but his... look, I know this is hard to hear, and I'm sorry, but his body was found at the carnival this morning, up on the Ferris wheel. We don't know how he got there, or why he went there in the middle of the night. Do you know anything that might help? Did he—or anybody—say anything around the neighborhood, while you were all hanging out, or anything? Maybe he was meeting someone, or mentioned sneaking into the carnival, something like that?"

I stared at him, and it was like everything else in the room went away, and there was just me and this cop's kind-eyed face hanging in space. Somewhere really far away I felt my mom take someone's hand; it might have been mine, I couldn't be sure. His *body* was found? That's what he'd said, not that *Tommy* was found, all whining and crying and spilling his guts, but that his *body* was found? What the hell had—

Suddenly, plastered across the old sad face, like one of those double exposures they used in movies, I saw Tommy the way I'd seen him last: just white-knuckled hands gripping the safety bar as the gondola rose into the night sky.

You were asleep and you don't know nothing, said Jerry's voice, all telephone distortion and controlled panic. *Remember that: you don't know nothing.*

"Son?" said the cop's face, and suddenly Tommy's pale fingers were gone and the world was back, with Dad, two cops, and Mom squeezing my hand like it had somehow done her wrong. Jerry's voice whispered through my head—*Remember that: you don't know nothing*—as I opened my mouth, and it took a couple of tries to shove some words out.

"I... I can't think of anything like that. We all... we all went to the carnival yesterday, for the whole day, and I don't think he said anything about going back. I mean, I planned to, like three or four more times. I saved all summer, and was rationing my money you know? Twenty bucks a trip, and I could go four times—or five, if I had any left over..."

I was babbling. The older cop knelt there, nodding and smiling, the younger stood behind him, notepad in hand but not writing anything down.

"So... uh... I guess that's just no," I said. "I really wish I could help, but I can't think of any—"

"I told you that's what he'd say!"

We all jumped, and when the young cop turned I could suddenly see her: Mrs. Taglioni standing in the doorway, not much taller than Tommy himself, tight-lipped and red-eyed, mascara running down her cheeks.

Her chest heaved like she'd just sprinted across the street—which she probably had.

"I *told* you that's what he'd say," she repeated, starting toward me like a small Italian landslide, pushing the younger cop aside and nearly bowling over the older one as he rose. Dad tried to step in her way, as he had with the cops, but she didn't slow, a force of nature in low heels bearing down on me. I shook Mom's hand loose and stood, determined that if this woman was going to dress me down, or maybe even kill me for what I'd done to her son, the least I could do was meet her on my feet.

Or maybe I was getting ready to run. It could've been that, too.

"Mrs. Taglioni, I—"

She was a stride away when her arms shot out, and my hands were suddenly trapped in a double iron grip. Mrs. Taglioni held me there, face-to-face, her red-rimmed, sorrow-filled eyes staring up into my wide, terrified ones. "You!" she said, then paused, swallowing, working at it like she was trying to down an ostrich egg whole, eyelids fluttering as she fought tears that, nonetheless, carried still more mascara down her cheeks.

If I'd had super speed, like some of my comic book heroes—The Flash, or Superman, or maybe Quicksilver— I'd have disappeared during one of those blinks. Just poof, gone, and spent the rest of my life living in Borneo or something. But I couldn't even take off at regular speed: it was like her grip on my hands had locked my feet to the floor, and all I could do was watch her swallow that lump and take in a great breath of air, ready now to really let me have it.

"You... you were always such a good friend to my Tommy, you and the other boys. He told me all the things you did together. I can't tell you how many nights he sat at the dinner table telling me about you, Ray, and Jerry, and the way you all took care of him. I never told him this, but I always imagined you three like the Musketeers in that story, with my little Tommy tagging along like young D'Artagnan. Thank you. Thank you for that. I told them you wouldn't know anything about this. I told them, but they still had to come over here with their *questions*." Her little face tightened, then crumpled. "Oh, God, what am I going to do without my Tommy? What am I going to do?"

With a two-fisted, whiplash-inducing jerk, she pulled me down into a hug, burying her face in my shoulder, tiny arms locked about my back, a constrictor snake dipped in old lady perfume. She cried into my chest, not like women do in the movies, but like a little kid, with great, wracking sobs. Guys in the movies always knew what to do when this happens, but the last weeping woman I'd dealt with had been when I was eleven, and my younger cousin had stubbed her toe playing tag. I couldn't see Mom, but Dad and the cops were all looking on with these lost expressions; I wasn't going to get any help there.

Not knowing what else to do, I put an arm around Tommy's mom, awkwardly patting her back in what I hoped was a comforting manner. *I'm going to hell for this*, I thought. Then the image of Tommy's white-knuckled fingers rising up and out of sight ran through my head again, and I supposed that maybe I was already in hell, that I'd taken some kind of express elevator down, just as Tommy had gone up, and I'd be spending eternity standing here feeling Mrs. Tagalong's tears soaking through my shirt while she thanked me for being such a good friend to her son.

CHAPTER 5

YOU SURE NOBODY'S HERE?

"What the hell did we do?"

Jerry glared. "We didn't do nothing. Right? That's what we told the cops, and Mrs. Taglioni backed us up. We didn't *do* nothing. We didn't do *nothing*." He nodded like he'd finally found the proper emphasis to put on the words, and I just stared. We were in his backyard, and it had been hours since the police had finally gotten me away from Mrs. Taglioni. I'd wanted to run right over to Ray's or Jerry's, but my parents had preferred to shut me in for the day; the cops were asking questions all over the neighborhood, and Mom and Dad just wanted me to stay out of the way.

It was a good thing I hadn't run right over, because Mrs. Taglioni had made stomping little trips to each of their houses to repeat her performance from my living room—though Jerry being Jerry, he'd seen her coming and managed to get into the bathroom, claiming something he called *emotional-intestinal distress*. He accepted her heartfelt thanks through the locked bathroom door as she clung, weeping, to one of the cops.

"You know what I mean," I said, looking about at the late afternoon shadows lengthening across Jerry's yard, paranoid about being overheard. I remembered that the last time I'd searched the shadows for unseen watchers, we'd been in the shadows, hiding at the base of the dark and silent Ferris wheel, and a surge of guilt pumped up my anger at Jerry's attitude. "We're the ones the cops are looking for. *We* got him to the carnival in the middle of the night. *We* got him up on that wheel." I looked straight at Ray. "And *we* were the ones who left him trapped up there."

I half expected Ray to take a swing at me, goaded by the accusation in my voice; part of me was actually hoping for it, needing the release of a good old-fashioned punch-up, even if I did lose. I was angry with them for getting me into this, angry with them for what they'd done in trapping Tommy up there, eventually killing him. It had all been Jerry's idea, after all, and then Ray had cut the starter rope. All I had done was...

All I had done was talk the kid into getting on the damn ride. I'd unlatched the bar and caught him when he'd stumbled. I'd closed the bar and given him the carny's remembered spiel like it was all a big joke—which it was supposed to be. Just a big joke.

All I'd done was tell him he'd be fine, then watch his terrified hands hold onto the safety bar and rise up into the night sky and right out of this world.

I'd told him he'd be *fine*.

But Ray didn't rise to the bait and give me the fight— the beating—part of me wanted. In fact, Ray barely seemed to be paying attention to the conversation, instead looking about the yard even more than I was. He spoke to Jerry as if he wasn't even aware I'd said anything. "You sure nobody's here?"

Jerry shrugged. "Sure, I'm sure. My mom wanted something nice to wear to the funeral, so Pop took her up to Ayres in Lafayette. I think he really went with her to make sure she doesn't spend too much money, but whatever. It's an hour drive each way, and Mom isn't a fast shopper."

"You sure?" Ray repeated, looking over his shoulder, toward the house.

"Yeah, I'm sure. What's up with you, man?"

"What's up with the *both* of you?" I said, and I had a hard time keeping my voice down. "Tommy *died*. We did that. He was a pain in the ass, yeah, but *we did that*. It's not a joke anymore. He's not coming back."

"You sure?" Ray said again, but he was still checking out the yard behind him, and I couldn't tell whether he was asking Jerry, or making fun of me.

"Yeah," I said, almost shouting now. "I'm sure. The cops said—"

"The cops," Jerry interrupted, "don't know why he was out there. We do. So what? They also want to know anything that'll help explain how he died. I can't explain that. Can you?" He pointed a finger at Ray, who looked startled at being addressed, like he still hadn't been paying attention. The finger pointed at me. "Can you? No. You can't. He was fine when he walked onto that wheel—under his own steam, nobody forcing him. You saw him. He was left alone for a while. So what? What, you think he died of exposure up there on a clear, seventy-five-degree night? Maybe his fat ass starved going three or four hours without a snack?"

"But his asthma—"

"Seemed fine to me. I mean, he wasn't wheezing at all, right? Quiet enough to sneak up on us, wasn't he?"

I flailed about in my head, looking for more stuff to point out. I knew this was all wrong, *knew* it, but Jerry kept making a weird kind of sense. I hadn't expected this: I knew we were guilty—*of course we were*—so how the hell had I gotten into an argument where I had to *prove* we were guilty? I took a last stab at it with the one thing that kept popping into my mind.

"He was wheezing more when he got on the wheel," I said. "You guys were too far away to hear him, but he was. And he was afraid of heights, right? So what if the thing took him up and he got scared, and his asthma—"

"He had his inhaler," said Jerry. "We all saw it. He was holding on to the thing like he wanted to marry it."

He was right—we'd all seen. I remembered Tommy clutching the thing as I caught him in his stumble, pressing it to his thigh as he tried to hold himself down to Earth. If his asthma had acted up, he hadn't even needed to fish the thing out of his pocket.

"You really think," said Jerry, like he was reading my thoughts, "he wouldn't have been sucking on that thing just as soon as he needed it?"

He would, I thought, *but there's something wrong here, something I can't put my finger on.*

"Look, guys," said Ray, breaking my train of thought. "I don't like talking about this out here in the open. Anybody could come up behind us and listen in, you know? We might not even see 'em coming."

"I told you—" Jerry started, but big Ray didn't want to listen.

"I don't care," he said, and he was suddenly red faced and a little wild about the eyes, like he was going to give Jerry that beating I'd been looking for earlier. "I don't like it. They could be right behind us and we wouldn't know it. I don't like it." He half-turned, scanning the yard, and Jerry and I exchanged a look. *Oh, sure*, that look said, *everything's going bad, but Ray's acting really weird, isn't he?*

"I'm out of here," Ray said, without turning back to us. "Next time we talk somewhere with a door we can close."

"Okay, Ray. Okay," said Jerry, shooting me the look again. "But remember, guys"—he raised his voice a little as Ray started for his own yard—"he was fine when we saw him, and we don't know what happened. We really don't." We watched Ray go, still looking about like a poorly trained movie spy searching for a tail. I murmured, "What's up with him?"

"What's up with *you?*" said Jerry.

"What's up with *me?*" I stared at him, feeling just how round my eyes were. "Haven't you been listening? Tommy die—"

"Tommy died. Yeah, I know. And yeah, like you said, it ain't a joke, and he ain't coming back. But there's nothing we can do about that, is there?"

I sputtered for a moment, my mouth wanting to make some point my head hadn't come up with yet.

"Nope," he continued. "Nothing we can do. But whatever we did or didn't do, the cops are looking to pin this on *someone.* You saw them, they were all over the neighborhood—someone could've robbed the bank this afternoon, no problem, because all the cops were on our street. This is the biggest thing to ever hit this neighborhood—cripes, my dad's driving a two-hour round trip to get my mom something to wear to a funeral for a kid they didn't even really know! This isn't the kind of thing that happens in a small town; this is big-city stuff."

He stepped closer, lowering his voice. "Whatever we did or didn't do, if you go talking to someone about it, they're gonna grab us, guilty or not. That'll mean jail. You want to go to jail for something we can't fix anyway?"

"We're thirteen," I said, fighting not to fall back a step. "They don't put thirteen-year-olds in jail."

"Reform school, then," he said. "Same difference. Reform school until we're eighteen, and then maybe jail.

That might be okay for you, though; you might make it. But what about Ray?"

That had come out of left field, and I finally did fall back a step. "What're you talking about?"

"His temper. You know how much trouble he'd get into every day without us here to watch out for him? A ton. You think they'd keep us all together in reform school? Then jail? He'd be in trouble every day. He'd never get out—if he survived."

Rather than taking a step forward—what I'd expected him to do when I stepped back—Jerry retreated a pace, waving a hand at himself. "What about me? Without you two around, I'm just the little guy. How do you think I'd do in reform school? I'd be the new kid, and half the size of everybody else. Daily beatings would be just the start of it." He shuddered. "And I don't even want to think about what would happen to me in prison."

"This is stupid," I said, backing away. I hadn't thought about any of this, but like everything else Jerry said, it made a weird kind of sense.

"Stupid would be thinking that feeling bad about Tagalong—and we really don't know what happened to Tagalong—would be a good reason to get all of us in trouble. Stupid would be thinking anything you do doesn't affect the rest of us. We're all in this together. Been like that since we were little, right? Like the Three Musketeers, right? All for one, and one for all?"

Without a word I turned to follow in Ray's footsteps, seeking my own yard. My own house. I wanted to make a retort, some kind of pithy exit line like you hear in the movies, but my head was spinning—spinning like a big, fast-moving Ferris wheel. Behind me, Jerry's voice rose to a hoarse almost-shout, like he was still trying to whisper.

"We don't even know what happened. We don't even know! We probably had nothing to do with it."

CHAPTER 6

ABOUT FIFTY PERCENT
PISS AND SPIT

We had everything to do with it.

Mom and Dad had managed to keep me from watching the local news that night, but Dad made the mistake of mentioning it was in the papers the next morning. I snuck out after breakfast and got the newspaper out of the bin, and there it was, in black and white.

Evidence of foul play, it said. A helpless young boy, it said. Acute respiratory distress brought on by stress, it said. And it mentioned Tommy's inhaler—except they called it a nebulizer—found not with the body, but lying at the base of the stalled wheel with the boy trapped nearly four stories away. How had this happened? the reporter wanted to know. Was it an accident, or by design? The police, the reporter claimed, could not answer his questions.

But I could.

We had everything to do with it, I thought again, pressing my face deeper into my tear-damp pillow.

It was both. Both by accident and by design. Jerry had planned to get Tommy up on that wheel, and Ray had known what he was doing when he killed the motor and cut the starter rope, but no one had planned on him losing his inhaler. We'd all seen him holding it, working it like my aunt June worked that worry stone of hers all the time. None of us had any clue he might've dropped it when we ran for the fence. None of us had known. How could we, with any noise the falling canister made hidden in the roar of the Ferris wheel's engine? How could we have known?

Except... I kind of *had* known, hadn't I?

I had known something was wrong when we were walking away—had even asked the guys if he'd be okay—but I hadn't been able to figure it out. Everybody was talking about Tommy's inhaler, saying he had it, he had it, but I'd been watching as that gondola rose into the night, and I had seen his hands—his noticeably empty-of-inhaler hands—holding on to that safety bar. Clutching it in sheer panic. He'd probably lunged to grab the bar just as soon as the ride had swung into motion—and what had I thought happened to any little thing he might've been holding?

I could see it now, whenever I closed my eyes: Tommy Tagalong, huddled in the exact center of the seat, pressing his hands to his thighs, just trying to maintain control and not bawl like a baby. He waited for the worst part of the nightmare to start, eyes squeezed tight behind those thick lenses, fingers working over that thing that was always with him—that was practically part of him—that had saved his life and kept him safe more than once.

Then the motor had started, and he'd really tensed up. And when the wheel started to turn, and that gondola jerked into motion, his eyes had jammed open like the lids were on springs and he'd lunged without a thought for the nearest thing he could hold on to. His hands had flown up and popped open as they went for the bar—and that inhaler had gone spinning off into the night. It hadn't needed to go far, just enough to clear the edge of the gondola. Just three or four feet. Three or four feet, and it might as well have been miles away, as far as Tommy was concerned.

We'd taken a trip once, my parents and me, to a little cottage on a lake—as close to camping as my mom would go. We don't have a lot of lakes here in Caina; the only other times I'd been swimming, not just fooling in a kiddy pool in the yard, was at the big pool at the YMCA. I went in there and splashed around and thought that was all there was to it: I had a handle on the whole swimming thing.

Then we'd gotten to the lake, and the first thing I'd done, while my parents were still unpacking the car, was whip off my shoes and shirt and run out onto the little dock floating in front of the house. I got to the end of that dock and jumped as high as I could, tucked my knees up so I could grab them, and came down in what I thought was going to be just the biggest cannonball on record in the state—maybe even the country.

Now, kiddie pools are small, and they warm up in the sun, and my dad says that public pool at the YMCA is about fifty percent piss and spit—which is why I don't go to the Y anymore—and it's indoors and heated. So, nothing I had ever done, not even the times I'd taken a shower right after Dad and the hot water had run out halfway through, had prepared me for the cold of a lake fed by rain runoff and mountain streams. My butt hit the surface with a slap, and an instant later the lake closed over my head—and that was when I discovered that water can be cold enough to hurt.

The shock hit, and I just couldn't help it. I gasped.

It was a good thing Dad had already been on his way over to yell at me about leaving them with all the unpacking, because I'm told he had me up and out of that water in less than a minute. I had to be told this, because I don't really remember it; all I remember is that thick feeling of icy water invading my lungs, and then them pulling and pulling but nothing happening as I strained to do something I'd never even had to think about before—and failing. The helplessness and terror filled me to overflowing as my whole world closed down to a pinpoint, and I focused on just that one thing: *breathe*.

Like I said, Dad got me out of the water and then the water out of me—I'm not sure how, exactly—while Mom stood by yelling at the both of us and crying. After I'd coughed out about a gallon of lake, the second thing Dad did was yell at me for scaring my mother like that, a job she took over when he had to walk away and catch his breath; but the first thing he did was sit on the ground with me, fully clothed and dripping, and hug me tight, rocking and crying.

That's what I kept thinking about now: that helpless terror. It had seemed like forever while it was happening, but it had only been a couple of minutes, tops, and for most of that I'd been up in the sunlight, surrounded by my family, someone doing their best to help me. What had it been like up on that wheel, alone in the dark, when the air stopped coming? Had he sat there, paralyzed with that same fear, lungs pulling but nothing happening, straining and failing at something the rest of us do every day without even really noticing? Or had he ignored the height in his panic, scrabbling around in the shadows of the gondola, looking for the one thing that could save him? The thing he never went anywhere without, that he'd had in his hand when he got on the ride? What had it been like when the breath never came, and the terror never left? What had killed him first, his useless lungs or the fear?

We had done that.

I spent the day in my room, and when I wasn't crying I felt like I was about to. Mom tried to coax me out for a while, then stood on the other side of the closed door telling me she was going to *give me some space*, and that it would *take some time*. I knew what she thought: that I was just upset at the loss of a friend and reading about it in the paper had made it worse.

She honestly had no idea.

I also knew when the guys heard what was in the news. I was lying on my bed, exhausted and half asleep, and suddenly Mom was there, lightly knocking on the door and telling me Jerry was on the phone. I told her I didn't want to talk right then and I'd call him later, but she was back in less than ten minutes to say Ray was on the phone. I told her again that I didn't want to talk, and I must have sounded pretty bad because she stopped bringing me the messages. I still heard the phone ringing all day, and sometimes I could hear Mom telling whoever was on the other end of the line that no, I still wasn't talking to anyone, and I'd get back to them as soon as I was up and about.

The doorbell rang a couple of times, too, and though she didn't come tell me, I found out later that it was the two of them, standing on our front stoop and looking worried. Mom thought they were worried about me, and said it showed real character that the two of them were able to put aside their own grief to come check on a friend, but I knew what was really going on: after our talk in Jerry's backyard, they were worried about what I might say to the cops.

Even *I* was worried about what I might say. But every time it got to be too much, that I thought I'd have to tell someone what we'd done or I'd just die, Jerry's words popped into my head. I couldn't just turn myself in, couldn't even say I was sorry, without turning them in, too. Ruining them. Destroying them, if Jerry was right. They were my best friends, had been all my life, and like Jerry'd said, there was nothing I—or we—could do to bring Tommy back. But the poor kid had been so alone...

It went on like that all day, and though my mother's protectiveness had always been kind of embarrassing in the past, I was thankful for it on that day. Realizing I was hurting (without, thank God, actually understanding why) and really wanted to be left alone, she set herself up like some kind of guardian, putting off all her usual errands and doing things around the house to be nearby if I needed anything. She was there whenever the doorbell or telephone rang, her own version of the protective wall my dad had been against the cops the day before.

God, I love my mom.

When Dad came home from work, he took over guard duty, and she must've told him about all the guys' calls, because I heard his response the next time the phone rang.

"I want to thank you boys for your concern, but I understand you've been calling all afternoon. Enough is enough. He'll call you back when he's ready to talk to you and not before, and until he does these calls stop now, are we clear? Good, because if this phone—or the doorbell—rings while I'm trying to eat dinner, I'm not even going to answer it. I'm just going to march right on over there and have a talk with both your parents. What? Well, you just better hope no one else calls then, shouldn't you? Yes. Yes, I'll tell him. Goodbye."

Thirty seconds later there was a knock at my door, gentler than you would have expected from the tone he'd just been using. I called a hello and my father came in, face concerned, but stern.

"That call was for you."

"Jerry or Ray?"

"Jerry. But Ray was in the background asking 'What'd he say? What'd he say?'" His eyes softened a bit. "Your mom says you read what was in the paper, and you're taking it pretty hard."

I nodded.

"Says you skipped lunch, just stayed in here all day moping."

"Yeah," I said. "Sort of."

"Well, look, you won't get over anything lying here starving yourself. You can come back in here afterward if you want to, but you're coming out for dinner. You're going to eat something and talk to your mom—you know, you really shouldn't worry her like this."

I almost smiled at that. "Okay, Dad, I'll try."

He gave me one hard, fast nod. "Good. You know, I kind of don't understand this. I was under the impression you didn't even like the Taglioni kid."

Any good feelings I had over my father's stern concern evaporated at that, and he must have seen the change in my face. He suddenly looked at the floor, rubbing the back of his neck, uncomfortable again. "Guess I must have been mistaken. Well. You just try to pull yourself together and put on a good show for your mother, all right? We'll get through this."

He was gone, closing the door quietly despite how quickly he left. I think it says a lot that, with everything that was going on, and the way I was acting, it never crossed his mind once that I might have had anything to do with it.

CHAPTER 7

IT WAS OPEN

My father's little talk with Jerry did the trick, and I lived in my room like a hermit (with the exception of mealtimes; Dad was pretty clear about that) for a whole 'nother day, and some of a third.

That was the day of the funeral.

"You're going." My father stood in my doorway, rigid, arms folded across his chest in roughly the same stance he'd used to face the cops who came to our door. There was still concern in his eyes, but his posture and tone said *enough is enough* as clearly as the words he'd spoken into the phone. "The whole neighborhood is going to be there, whether they knew this kid or not, and you've been in here moping for two days now. If you're that upset about his... his passing, then I think you'd want to be there to say a last goodbye."

"But I—"

"You're going. You've grown, but see if you can wedge yourself into your suit—if not, you can borrow one of mine. It'll be too big for you, but at least you'll be able to breathe."

I winced.

I struggled into my suit—it was tight, but I'd been uncomfortable in it even when Dad said it was a perfect fit—and we left for the church. I stuck close to Mom and Dad and just tried to be invisible, pretending not to hear people's greetings if I could, worrying the whole time that someone might ask if I knew anything, or try to console me over the loss of my friend. I saw Jerry and his parents—his mother in a spiffy new dress from Ayres—but they'd gotten there early and had close to front-row seats. My father had been right when he said the whole neighborhood would be there, and I'd made us late trying not to go; we barely made it into the last row before it became standing room only.

Mom and Dad were a little upset by that, but the more distance I could keep between the guys and me, the better—I don't think I could have taken their searching looks, or Jerry trying to corner me for another reform school lecture. I looked around for Ray, and when I saw his parents, close to the front but sitting without him, I panicked. I kept scanning the people around us, convinced Ray was about to step out of the crowd and clap a hand on my shoulder like a cop in some old movie pinching a crook. It wasn't until the service was about to start that I realized he hadn't just stepped away from them; his parents had come to the funeral without him.

That seemed ominous, but before my worry could gain any steam, all attention in the church was drawn to the front. Father Wilson stood in the pulpit, ready to begin. He wasn't speaking yet, just waiting for everyone to notice his presence at the lectern and quiet down—and except for Mr. and Mrs. Salome, an old couple from up the block who wouldn't admit they were practically deaf, we had. Father Wilson gave it another minute, to let the people around the shouting couple tell them it was about to start—and that was when I heard it, the only sound left in the church besides Mr. Salome's "What? What?"

Mrs. Taglioni, sitting in the center of the front row, was sobbing.

She had wept like a broken-hearted child when she'd come to my house, and according to the guys she'd cried the whole time she had been to each of their houses too. *How could she still be crying?* I wondered. *Wouldn't she run out of tears? Why hadn't she run out of tears?* But we had learned in science class that year about the human body, and how it's really mostly water. Was that where all her tears came from? Would she just cry and cry, using up the stuff she was made of until she finally disappeared?

I pictured a weeping Mrs. Taglioni growing smaller, shrinking out of her clothes like the guy in that Richard Matheson book, and I think I smiled. Hell, I almost laughed. But as the Salomes finally quieted down and I listened to Mrs. Taglioni go on, I felt my face, smiling or not, go wooden.

It had been three days, but she sounded just the same as she had in our living room: just as heartbroken, and sobbing just as hard. Maybe harder. Was it ever going to get better for her? Or was it going to be like the story in that Matheson book, where the guy shrank a little each day until he disappeared? I didn't think she was going to cry herself into a different dress size, but maybe inside, where no one could see, she'd get a little smaller every day. A little... I don't know. Sadder. Deader.

"We have come together today," Father Wilson began, "to celebrate a life cut tragically short..."

That was all I heard. I didn't catch the rest of what he said—I don't even know if he kept talking—because right then, as he mentioned *cut tragically short*, he gestured to his right, and for the first time I saw the casket lying in front of the rail. I had known it was there—this was a funeral, for Christ's sake—but I hadn't looked at it. There had been a dark spot, a black thing in the front of the room, but my eyes had skittered away like beads of water on a hot skillet. They had had other things to do, like avoid people's eyes, scan the church for Ray, even watch Mrs. Taglioni's shuddering shoulders. Now, though, because of an almost casual gesture Father Wilson made, simply pointing out why we were all there, I looked at the casket.

It was open.

Tommy Taglioni lay there, eyes closed, peaceful looking, and very, very dead. I might have thought he was sleeping—that happens sometimes in movies and books, someone makes that mistake—except for his perfect coloring. Where you could always identify Wheezy Taglioni from a block away by his cheeks, all red and blotchy from the effort of breathing, this face was tan and smooth looking. His glasses weren't on, and so I might've thought he looked like someone else, but no one else in the neighborhood was that short and fat; I guess there wasn't anything they could do about that at the funeral home.

Only the top half of the casket was open, but what I could see of his belly rose like it was trying to get out of the box before disappearing beneath the lower lid. That collar of flesh around his neck was still there, too, the place I'd seen the shadow dance as he swallowed his fear and looked up at the darkened Ferris wheel. His face looked oddly naked without its glasses, and though I knew I must've seen him without them a dozen times, maybe more—he'd had to clean the damn things, hadn't he?—all I could think of was slapping him on the back as I told him to shit or get off the pot and his Coke-bottle lenses slipping down his nose to show me his frightened little eyes.

Everything about him reminded me of that night at Dingaling Brothers'. I clenched my hands together in my lap, just as he had while I'd given him the carny's speech, and I was glad Tommy's hands were down beside him now, in the coffin and out of sight rather than crossed on his chest: if I could have seen his fingers, and imagined them suddenly curling into the white-knuckled claws that rose away from me into the night sky, I would've started screaming, and if I started, I might never have stopped.

I imagined it, heard my own terrible screeching—and the people around me flinched and looked at each other. For an instant I thought I *had* screamed aloud, and then the horn sounded. I realized I hadn't heard myself at all, but tires screeching across asphalt. The blast of the car horn stopped, but in its place someone was shouting, yelling for help, and some of the people around me were on their feet and shuffling rapidly between the pews.

My father was one of those on his feet. He gestured at me and Mom with a quick "Stay here!" before he pushed into the crowd filling the aisle. I glanced at Mom, saw her watching my father's retreating back, and I launched myself forward. Her fingers grazed the back of my shoulder, she shouted "No," but she was too slow to stop me as I slipped into Dad's wake. He bulled his way through the people and I stayed right on his tail. A log jam of bodies filled the church doorway but, sitting in the back of the church as we had, my father was toward the front of the clog; as he got stuck in the press, I squirted out between him and another black suit and made it to the front steps. He called me back, but I ignored him, urged down the wide granite stairs by a horrible suspicion.

St. Michael's was only four blocks from our house but was around the corner on much busier Main Street. Traffic was stopped in both directions at a spot a half a block from the church. It was easy to find: maybe the horn had gone silent, and the yelling had died down, but one man stood beside a car at the center of the frozen vehicles shouting, "I didn't see him! He ran out of nowhere, right in front of me—I couldn't stop! I tried! I tried!"

A crowd was growing around the car—people in dark suits and dresses from the church, others in their shirtsleeves from the stopped cars—but only one person lay in the street, arms and legs flopped about in a way that looked uncomfortable, neck bent at an angle that looked impossible, the crown of his head resting on the ground even though he was lying flat on his back.

Ray's eyes were open, and round, and he stared at me, upside down, as I stood between a pair of strangers, staring back. His mouth was open incredibly wide, the rest of his head pulled back like a Pez dispenser by the impact, or the tarmac, or maybe it was what it looked like: that Ray had died in the middle of a long and terrible scream. Even without the mortician's makeup and the fancy box, Ray looked just as dead as Tommy. He lay just as still, nothing but the end of his tie moving, fluttering slightly in the breeze. I noticed his hands, one open wide, the other curled into a loose version of one of his usual fists. The arm leading to the wide-open hand, I saw, seemed to have two elbows. Or maybe that bend in his forearm was a new wrist?

I made a sound deep in my throat that felt like a growl, though it sounded more like a whimper. The man beside me tore his attention from the sight of one of my best friends lying dead in the street to look over and see me for the first time. "Hey, kid," he said. "Don't look at that. You don't wanna see that."

One of the men by the car looked up at his words, gazed across Ray's broken body and saw me standing there, then looked around and went a little wide eyed, as if realizing for the first time there were women and children in the crowd. He yanked off his suit coat and knelt, spreading the jacket out with a little flourish and letting it settle over Ray, hiding his fluttering tie and Pez dispenser head.

That left arm, with its new elbow—or was it a wrist?—stuck out from beneath the makeshift covering like a twisted jackstraw.

Strong hands grabbed my shoulders, spun me roughly about, and my vision was filled with my father's pale and angry face. "I told you to stay with your mother," he started, but from the crowd of people spilling down the church steps behind him, a small figure popped into view, slipping through the crush as easily as he had the people at the carnival, quickly outdistancing his parents who were probably still trapped in the front of the church.

"Is it Ray?" Jerry shouted. "It's Ray, isn't it?"

My father looked past me, to the coat-covered shape on the ground, and stiffened as he realized just what I'd seen before his arrival. His expression didn't change except for a slight squint, and he made a sound that probably started out as a gasp, but he'd managed to cut down to just a slight hiccup; his grip on my shoulders loosened, though, his hands frozen but no longer squeezing.

"It's Ray, isn't it?" Jerry repeated, but I was already slipping free of my father and turning away. Dad's fingertips brushed the back of my shoulder, just like Mom's had, but it was too late. And though he'd always been the fastest of us, even Jerry couldn't catch me as, tight suit and dress shoes be damned, I ran for home.

CHAPTER 8

WE HAVE TO TALK

The next morning Dad didn't even mention the newspaper, but I'd heard it rustling in the bathroom after his shower and knew we had one; that he didn't read it at the breakfast table like always meant there was something in there he didn't want me to see. After working halfway through a plate of pancakes, I slipped into the garage while Mom and Dad said goodbye at the door, and fished out the paper Dad had jammed into the bin. I snuck down the hall to my room—the meal was over, I could go back to being a hermit again—before Mom would see I'd been in the garage, and quietly flipped the paper open.

SECOND DEATH OF LOCAL BOY

There was a statement from Ronald Burgess, the driver, saying pretty much what he'd been shouting at the scene: Ray had come running out of nowhere, and though he'd tried to stop, it'd been too late. A police detective named Howard said the scene of the accident appeared to support Burgess's story: skid marks indicated he'd tried to stop, and that he hadn't been speeding. The reporter speculated that Ray had been despondent over the death of his good friend, one Thomas Taglioni, and had been on his way to Taglioni's funeral as indicated by his shirt and tie.

I stopped reading for a minute, my tears blurring the words on the page as I remembered Ray's tie fluttering in the breeze. I hadn't realized it at the time, but Ray had been dressed to go to the funeral. Why hadn't he been there? Was I not the only one consumed with guilt? Had Ray, on his way to say goodbye to the boy we had killed, seen a way out from under that guilt? A way that wouldn't affect me and Jerry the way a confession would have? Had he—

There was a sudden sound from my open window, a quick, sharp *pssst*. I glanced at the window—and with a shout I slipped sideways from my seat on the edge of my bed, tumbling to the floor.

Mom was knocking at my door in seconds. "Are you okay?"

"I'm fine," I called. "I just slipped."

"Are you sure?"

"Yes, I'm sure I slipped. Sorry I scared you."

After a moment I heard her move off down the hall toward the front of the house, and I turned to the window, where Jerry's face pressed close to the screen.

"We have to talk," he said.

"Why wouldn't you take my calls?" he sat on the end of my bed as I quietly slid the screen back down. "I kept calling, and your mom said—"

"It was our fault," I interrupted.

Jerry didn't even try to look confused. Instead he shot right past confused to denial.

"Hey, we didn't make him toss his nebu-whatsis over the side, did we? We didn't even know he did it. If we had, sure, we would've gotten him down from there, or gone for help or something. But we didn't know, did we?"

"No, but we—"

"And what kind of a dumbass throws away stuff that'll keep him alive? What's that about?" Jerry's wide-eyed expression of innocence looked a little bit ridiculous if you knew him, and he was talking too slowly, overenunciating like he was trying to convince himself as much as anyone else. He threw in an exaggerated shrug, his shoulders nearly covering his ears. "It was his own carelessness, you ask me."

"His own carelessness?" I loomed over him—not hard, what with Jerry being so small and sitting down, besides. "*We* got him up there. *We* got him out there in the first place! *We*—"

I'd started getting louder, and Jerry leaned back, palms raised. "Hey, hey," he said. "Easy. Your mom's gonna hear, you keep shouting like that." He looked me up and down, then added—again in his over-casual tones— "You, uh, you feeling all right?"

"I—"

"Besides, we already gave the cops our stories about that, and we're sticking to 'em. I'm here to talk about Ray."

Part of me had been relieved to have Tommy to talk about, to keep my mind busy, but now a memory of Ray's upside-down eyes hit me. His wide-open mouth. His broken jackstraw arm. My legs felt like water for a second, and I steered myself to a seat on the bed. I'd cried about it the night before, but right at that moment, thinking about Ray on the heels of being so mad with Jerry, all I managed was a strange sort of numbness.

"Jesus, I wonder what happened," I whispered.

"I know what happened," said Jerry.

I stared at him. "You were in the church."

"Well, okay," he shrugged again. "I don't *know* know, but I know, you know?"

"What the hell are you talking about?"

"That's what I was calling—" he started, but broke off suddenly, looking at the window. Then he popped off the bed and was across the room, pressing an ear to the door. I hadn't heard anything, but Mom wore her slippers inside the house, and whether she meant to be or not, she could be pretty stealthy sometimes. He listened for a long moment, then crept back. He shot a glance at the window again as he sat, leaning in to take his whispering more seriously.

"That's what I was trying to call you about. Well, one of the things, anyway, when Ray wasn't right there with me."

"What are you talking about?"

"I'm talking about Ray," he said. "You saw him the other day, right? I mean, was he acting normal to you?"

I thought about Ray, more interested in keeping an eye on everything than the conversation, constantly checking over his shoulder out in the middle of the yard and practically whispering. Not even noticing I was spoiling for a fight. None of that sounded like Ray, and I shook my head.

"I didn't think so either," said Jerry. "And after that he got worse. I mean, you know Ray: guy wasn't usually worried about who might see what, you know? He wasn't all that aware of consequences."

I remembered having to point out to Ray that beating up the neighborhood cripple might not be seen as a good thing but didn't say anything. I didn't have to: Jerry was on a roll.

"But ever since that night at the wheel he was all jumpy. Always looking over his shoulder, asking if I'd heard anything. Asking if we were alone when we were *obviously* alone. I mean, you couldn't talk to the guy where he wasn't interrupting the whole time, checking doors and windows. You remember how he asked that the next time we all got together we did it inside, where we could keep things private, something like that?"

I nodded. "Next time we talk somewhere with a door we can close."

"Yeah, that's it. Well that didn't fix things. Seemed like that made it worse. He said anyone could sneak up on you outside, but inside he just kept looking around—sometimes even behind the furniture. It was really starting to weird me out, but I was kind of afraid to say anything, you know? I mean, he wasn't acting exactly normal, and he walked around ready to take a swing at you on a *good* day. If something set him off and he decided to pound on me, you wouldn't have been there to calm him down, you know what I mean?"

I did know—in fact, I was the one who'd pointed it out to Jerry: the three of us were like some kind of balancing act, with the two of us keeping Ray in check. When they'd taught us about dinosaurs in school, they'd said something about the dinos' little brains, and that they probably couldn't keep track of more than one thing at once—they could hunt one animal to eat, but if there were two or three and they split up, the dinosaur would get confused and the prey could escape. I'd told Jerry that made me think of Ray: he'd get all worked up in a heartbeat and decide to whip the tar out of one of us, but as long as the other was there to distract him, he'd forget about being mad in a minute and things would go back to normal; the prey escaped.

We were all best friends, but neither of us were really too keen on hanging around with Ray one-on-one. It was just a little dangerous, especially inside where Jerry couldn't have run away.

"I thought he was worried about his parents being nosy," he said. "But I didn't say anything. Just helped him look through windows and stuff, even though there was never anyone there. He made me nervous as hell, but I couldn't *not* go over there—I was worried about him, you know?

"Then, the other day—the day before the funeral—I couldn't take it anymore. He'd pulled a kitchen chair into his room and he was sitting there with his back to the wall where he could see both the door and window, but he was still looking over his shoulder, like he was expecting someone to be there. 'Ray,' I said. 'Seriously, man, you're freaking me out. What're you looking for?'"

Jerry sat there for a couple of seconds just looking at me, and I finally spread my hands and raised my eyebrows, bobbing my head forward in the universally recognized sign for *Well?*

"Tagalong," he whispered. "He said he was looking for Tagalong."

A cold, crawly feeling settled into my stomach. "What are you talking about? Tommy's dea—"

"I know Tagalong's dead," Jerry said, whispering so hard it seemed like a shout. "*Ray* knew Tagalong was dead, but he was still looking for him."

"Why?"

"It was all jumbled up—Ray was really upset, and I don't think he'd been sleeping too good—but he said Tagalong was back. Don't look at me like that! That's what he said!"

"He saw him?"

"I... don't think so. I dunno. I told you, it was all— this is Ray we're talking about, he wasn't big on making sense, but the kid was really scared, and... that's what really had me freaked out."

"What?"

"This was Ray, you know?" said Jerry. "This was Ray, talking about something that scared him spitless, you could tell, but he didn't get mad. Not at all. He was just... scared. That's why I think I know what happened yesterday."

My head was spinning with his story—and if he was right, then yeah, Ray not getting mad about being scared might have been the weirdest thing about all of this.

"What are you talking about?"

"Ray was terrified, man. I mean, he called me yesterday when his parents started ordering him to the funeral. He didn't want to go."

"Neither did I," I said. "That's why we were so late."

"You *didn't want* to go. Ray was petrified. He'd spent a couple of days thinking he was being followed by Tagalong, he said there was no way he was going to go visit the kid! When he got off the phone I could already hear his dad in the background telling him he was going, but then they showed up at the funeral without him. They sat near us, and they were all polite smiles and everything, but you could tell they weren't too happy. I listened when they whispered to each other, and I think they almost got Ray there, but at the last second he locked himself in the bathroom or something."

He made a face and shook his head.

"That guy in the paper had it all wrong. There was no way Ray was running to the funeral. I mean, even if he was, you don't have to cross Main Street to get there anyway. What was he doing in the road?"

I realized he was right; I'd run all the way home from the church, and I never crossed Main Street once.

"You know what I think? I think he was running from something." He leaned closer, dropping his voice into an intense stage-whisper. "I think he was running from Tagalong."

"So, what," I said. "You think the thing with Tommy made him crazy or something? Like the guilt drove him nuts?"

"I dunno." He glanced at the window again. "I don't... look, you haven't seen anything weird, have you?"

The footsteps in the hall probably weren't as sudden as they seemed—Jerry and I were just so deep in the conversation we didn't hear Mom coming until she was right outside—but by the time I heard her step to the other side of the door, Jerry had practically levitated off the bed, eyes huge and ready to run. Forget the always-thinking Jerry I knew, supremely confident in his ability to slip through trouble like some slick-talking ghost; I think if I hadn't grabbed his arm he might have tried to dive right through the window screen like some ninety-pound action hero.

Mom knocked. "Lunch is ready."

"Okay," I called back as Jerry hunkered behind my bed in case she opened the door. "I'll be right there."

"Don't be long," she said, voice fading as she moved back down the hall. "It's grilled cheese. Get 'em while they're hot!"

I listened for a moment to make sure she was gone, then looked down at Jerry, still squatting between the bed and window. "What is your *problem*?" I whispered.

"I just don't want to get caught," he whispered back. "I'm supposed to be in my room. I was in there for a while with the radio on, you know, trying to avoid the parents, but being alone was bad. Worse than I thought. So I locked the door, turned up the volume, and snuck out the window."

"Wait," I said. "Worse than what?"

He ignored my question. "Can't you skip lunch or something?"

I shook my head. "Dad mandated spending mealtimes with him and Mom, so they know I'm okay."

"Aw, man." To my surprise, slick little Jerry looked pretty upset—close to tears, if I didn't know any better. "I just... you know... don't want to be alone, I guess."

"Getting cold out here," Mom called from the kitchen.

"What is with you?" I said. "Look, why don't you just come eat? Go around to the front door and invite yourself in for lunch? It's not like you haven't done that bef—"

"I don't want my mom getting wind I was out of the house. If they figure I went out through the window I could get grounded, and that'd put me all alone for a while—or with just them to talk to, and I can't talk to them about him."

"About who?" I said, confused. "Ray?"

"Tagalong!" he stage whispered through gritted teeth.

"Now, please!" Mom called.

I crossed the room and put my hand to the doorknob. "Stay here, then. I'll be back as soon as I can—but what about Tommy?"

Footsteps started up the hall toward my room; I guess Mom was tired of waiting. As I turned the knob to dart out and head her off, Jerry shot a quick glance over his shoulder at the open window—probably thinking about escaping, that was so like him—then back to me. "I don't think Ray was nuts."

Those six words echoed in my head as I stepped out into Mom's path, trying not to seem like I was slamming the door behind me.

"I was calling you," she said.

"And here I am." I spread my arms slightly, as if showing her me in all my glory—and also blocking her path to my door. "You said something about grilled cheese?"

I followed her to the kitchen where I choked down a lunch I didn't really want, glad I hadn't been very talkative at mealtimes lately; my being lost in thought wasn't all that unusual. I spent the first half of the sandwich thinking about the last thing Jerry'd said: *I don't think Ray was nuts.*

Jerry was smart—and more than smart, he was... oh, what's the word, the kid didn't believe in anything... cynical! More than smart, Jerry was cynical. Ray and me, we'd talk about stuff like UFOs, and Area 51, and Heinlein's *Stranger in a Strange Land*, and that guy who'd been on television telling people he could bend spoons with his mind—Uri whatshisname—and Jerry would always make fun of us. UFOs were swamp gas and ball lightning, Area 51 was Uncle Sam letting people look for what wasn't there while he covered up the real stuff, *Stranger* was just fiction, and the guy with the spoons was a genius for taking in so many gullible people—like me and Ray.

But Ray had been saying some pretty crazy things, hadn't he? I mean, I hadn't heard him, but according to what Jerry'd said he sounded nuttier than a fruitcake. How could he think Ray wasn't nuts? And the last time I'd actually seen Ray—

Then it clicked. The whole time Jerry had been whispering in my room, he'd seemed a little off, but sort of familiar, like somebody quoting lines from a movie that you can't quite place. Right then, though, thinking of that last time we'd all been together, I realized where that familiar feeling had come from. Jerry kept looking over his shoulder, checking the window, just like Ray had been constantly checking behind him while we'd talked. Jerry had looked at the door, too, but that had made sense: he was worried about Mom. But the window? He'd looked at the window more than the door. What was he looking at the window for?

And that led to another thought: as big a deal as Jerry had made of Ray not getting mad over being scared—and it *was* a big deal, he was right about that—I could make the same point about how rattled Jerry'd been when my mom came to the door. Jerry didn't *get* rattled—or if he did, he never showed it—but he was sure showing it now.

All these thoughts kind of crashed together for me in a single, startling question: Had Jerry seen something?

I rolled it over and over in my head as I tore through the rest of my sandwich, washing down bread and cheese with mouthfuls of milk without really tasting anything. The more I thought about it, the weirder it all seemed, and I waited for my chance to get out of that kitchen and back to Jerry without Mom stopping me for a heart-to-heart.

Then she went into the living room for something, and I was up and out of my chair, quietly putting my cup and plate in the sink, barely making a sound as I speed-walked up the hallway in my socks. Jerry's last statement echoed in my brain as I turned the knob and slipped into my room: *I don't think Ray was nuts.* I wanted Jerry to explain that, and I wanted him to do it now.

Jerry wasn't hunkered behind my bed where I'd left him, nor was he under it. I checked the closet, recalling more than one time that he'd popped unexpectedly out of it with a high-pitched "Boo!" but all I found were clothes, shoes, and a few toys I'd put in there during my recent self-incarceration. I finally checked the window screen; I'd made sure both latches were fastened when I'd closed it after pulling Jerry in, but only the left-hand latch was closed now, the screen just a hair cockeyed in the frame.

I'd only been in the kitchen ten minutes or so, but in that time Jerry, afraid to be alone and acting a little paranoid, had exited the house the way he'd gotten in, and was gone.

CHAPTER 9

THIS ONE WAS ALL MINE

I spent the rest of the day wondering about Jerry and waiting to hear from him again. I thought about going over to talk to him, but what if he hadn't gone home? What if I rang the doorbell and sent his mom to knock on his bedroom door, but all that was in there was a radio with the volume turned up and a cockeyed window screen? I couldn't go get him in trouble like that—it would be majorly uncool. Same problem if I tried the phone.

I thought about sneaking over there the way he'd come over here, but if I didn't find him I couldn't get back into my room. Jerry could climb like a monkey—maybe it had to do with him being so small—and could do stuff like cling to the sill right outside my window like he had. He could get up and through his own window without help, but I needed him or Ray to give me a boost to get back into my own room—when I snuck out at night, I was quietly creeping through the back door.

I tried staying near the phone, in case he called, but if I thought Mom had been worried about me after Tommy was found, she was twice as bad now. I thought part of it was that she'd known Ray as long as I had—we'd pretty much grown up together—and so she was having a harder time with it than when it had just been the kid who'd moved in across the street a couple of years ago. Even Dad had seemed different when he'd gotten home from the church last night, silent and grim at the dinner table. He hadn't batted an eye when I ate fast, cut dinner short, and retreated to my room again.

So, while I could tell that today Mom was trying to leave me alone, to give me some space, after the tenth time she asked if I was okay I gave up on the idea of hanging out in the living room and resigned to just rushing out whenever the phone rang—and it rang a lot. Everything had been in the papers, and my whole family had known Ray. Already primed by what had happened with Tommy, my mom got calls from both my nana and grandma, as well as the aunts on Dad's side.

If I went out there while Mom was on the phone she insisted I at least say hi—but that was never all they wanted. Everyone I talked to asked how I was doing, how I was feeling, and it wasn't like I could just come right out and say *guilty, confused, and afraid*. Those calls were bad enough, but Mom's brother Danny, the uncle I'd worked for all summer, had gotten to know Jerry and Ray pretty well: they'd stopped by the shop every day I'd worked. Though it had gotten to the point that my eyes always felt hot and swollen, but stayed dry, hearing Uncle Danny obviously trying not to let me know he was crying flipped some switch in me and I started in, too. That was when I quit, told Mom I only wanted to talk to Jerry, and locked myself in my room again—and that was when *I* found out that now I had a problem with being alone.

Without Mom to occupy my mind with her nervous talk I had nothing to distract me from my own thoughts, and I wasn't my own best company right then. Up until Jerry'd come to invade my room, I'd been kind of numb about Ray, unable to process everything. Now, though, aside from the sadness and horror of the situation, Jerry had added to something else I was pretty lousy at handling: guilt.

It was almost worse than the guilt about what we'd done to Tommy—in that, at least, I'd been the one asking if he'd be okay. Jerry'd made me feel better about that—Jerry and that damn way he had of talking stuff around to his way of seeing things that was so hard to argue with. What had happened to Tommy I shared with Jerry and Ray: this one was all mine.

They'd been calling, and I'd ignored them. Turned my back on them over what had happened at the Ferris wheel, even though, like Jerry'd said, I was just as deep in that as they were, just as much at fault. They'd both been calling—and Jerry had been calling for help part of the time. He'd been trying to handle big Ray all on his own, one leg pulled out from under our little balancing act and leaving him to stagger around, trying not to let Ray fall.

Ray may have been calling for help too. I'd never know.

And I'd known Ray was off, hadn't I? Jerry and I'd exchanged that look in his yard because Ray wasn't acting like Ray. Just like my seeing Tommy's hands hanging onto that bar as he rose into the night sky was a clue I'd either missed or ignored, that scene in Jerry's backyard should've tipped me off that something was really wrong with Ray. We were best friends. I should have known.

What kind of a person was I, who could see these things and not know them for what they were? Was I stupid? Or was it that somewhere, deep inside, I understood them, but didn't care?

Hours later, after all my silent wondering, when the phone rang and Mom tapped on my door, a pit opened in my stomach. There was only one other person left in this mess, and if he walked away from me because I'd been being a jerk, then I really *would* be alone.

"Hello?"

"Hi."

At the sound of his voice I covered the mouthpiece with a hand and shouted, "Got it, Mom!" My mother hung up the phone in the living room as I started playing out the handset cord from the wall phone in the kitchen. At thirteen years old, there was no way my father was letting me have a phone in my room, but the phone in the kitchen had an extra-long cord so Mom could talk while cooking dinner and stuff. If I stretched it out enough, untangling the stupid springy thing as I went, I could get the handset into the bathroom and wedge the door shut. Dad always yelled at me for hogging the john and liked to point out that if I broke the cord I was paying for it, but I was pretty sure he'd let some things slide at the moment.

Besides, it was the only way to get any privacy on the phone in this house.

"What happened to you?" I whisper-shouted just as soon as I figured the door was wedged tight enough. "I thought you were going to wait in my room?"

"I couldn't," Jerry said softly, and he sounded miserable. "I thought maybe I could, you know? Like your room was different than my room, so maybe being in there for a while wouldn't be as bad, you know what I mean?"

"Sure," I said, then: "Well, not exactly. Okay, no, I don't know what you're talking about. What's your problem with being alone—and what did you mean about you don't think Ray was nuts? Seriously, man, I'm starting to worr—"

"That's what I was trying to tell you when you left. Ray was talking some crazy stuff, I know. You weren't there to hear him, man—I was."

There it was: the accusation. I closed my eyes, as if by not seeing the world I could keep anything out there from touching me, but it didn't do any good: the guilt was already inside; all closing my eyes did was trap me in there with it.

A couple of seconds later I realized Jerry was still talking. He hadn't even paused to put extra emphasis on the words—he wasn't making an accusation, just stating facts. I opened my eyes and caught up with the conversation, and now that I was paying attention I thought with a little thrill that *not* driving that home, *not* taking advantage of my guilt—which he'd know I was feeling—was not like Jerry at all.

"... was seriously worried that he'd lost it, you know? I was really freaked out, even thought about telling his mother or something."

That grabbed my attention. "Are you kidding me? You were the one so dead set on us not going to anyone."

"Hey, what else was I gonna do? The kid was falling apart right in front of me. I mean, it was all confused, but it sounded like he was seeing things, you know? I thought he was hallucinating or something... I didn't realize..."

"Didn't realize what?" I said, but I knew where he was going with this, and I wasn't going to like it.

"I don't think Ray was crazy," he whispered, so low I barely heard him, and my stomach dropped even further.

"You said that before," I murmured, losing the stage whisper—it sounded too accusing. "What did you mean? Ray was hearing voices, right, so—"

"I only *though*t he was hearing voices." He'd jumped into the harsh, whispering almost-shout I'd just abandoned, and I was right, it sounded accusatory—self-accusatory. "Ray wasn't explaining things well, and I thought he was hearing voices. He wasn't, though, and now

I *know* he wasn't. It's almost worse. But if he was, that means *I'm* crazy, too."

All I heard for a moment was thick, rapid breathing. I waited a heartbeat, then two, and was about to say something—I don't know what, anything to cover that awful breathing—when he whispered again, almost as quietly as before, and the tone in his voice, the despair coming from another thirteen-year-old, left butterflies of ice twiddling their wings along my spine. "I don't want to be crazy. I don't want to be crazy—but it might be better. Might be better to be crazy. I could go to a doctor, get some pills, get some shocks like in the movies, make it stop—"

"Jerry, what are you talking about?" I said, not murmuring now, maybe even a little louder than normal, because whether he answered or not I just had to stop him from saying what he was saying, had to stop him using that terrible, awful voice. "You're talking in circles, but I still don't know what you're talking about. How was Ray not crazy? If he wasn't hearing things, then what was... what's going on?"

"He's back." Jerry's voice hadn't changed—if anything, it was even softer and hollower than before. "He's back, and he's there, everywhere I go. Everywhere."

There was silence, nothing but us breathing at each other. I didn't want to break it this time, didn't want to ask the question that popped into my head. I knew what he was going to say, but two little words forced themselves out in a whisper, in the useless hope that he'd say something—anything—other than what I was expecting. "Who's back?"

"Tagalong."

My eyes closed again and I sagged sideways, resting a shoulder against the wall, head bent forward until my forehead was pressed to the cool painted surface of the bathroom door. Was crazy contagious? I didn't want to know the answer, wanted instead to hang up the phone and pretend none of this had ever happened—but that was how Jerry had wound up on the other end of this line, and how Ray had wound up in front of that car, wasn't it?

And besides... what if crazy wasn't catching? This was cynical Jerry, the kid who didn't believe in anything. What had...?

"You've seen him?" I whispered.

"Seen him? No." Jerry made a sound that might have been a laugh, and his voice rose from a whisper. "No, you never *see* him! I *wish* I could see him! Then maybe this thing would be over. But no, you don't get to see him, he's just *there*, and you *know* it, and there ain't a thing you can do about it. But I think I got him. I think I know a place he won't go, and—"

The door under my forehead suddenly shuddered with a brisk knock, and I fell back with a little shriek as my dad's voice came from the hallway. "You're not the only one who might need the bathroom, you know—and if you break this cord, young man, don't you think for a second that I'm going to pay for it!"

"I'll be out in a minute!" I shouted, fright pulling a tone from me I'd never dared use with my father before. He was silent for a beat. "Your mother says dinner's ready," he said, voice stiff, before I heard him stomp down the hall. When I put the receiver back to my ear, though, all I heard was a dial tone. Whether in fright at my dad's sudden voice, or thinking I was about to get in trouble anyway, Jerry had hung up. Quick as I could I dialed him back... and got a busy signal.

I pounded to the kitchen to hang up the phone and tried to keep right on going out the door, but my father was having none of it.

"You sit down right now and eat your dinner."

"But I just need to talk to Jerry for a—"

"Wasn't that Jerry you were just talking to?" His voice was hard with a combination of accusation and sarcasm, and I knew he was smarting from the tone I'd used.

"Yes."

"Seems to me you might have said all you needed to say right there."

"But, Dad—"

"Don't 'But, Dad,' me. You sit down right there, right now. Anything that's happened since you hung up that phone can wait until after dinner."

I knew there was no way around it, other than simply ignoring him and running out anyway—and that would have consequences I didn't even want to think about. I was too young to join the French Foreign Legion, and apart from that I couldn't think of a place I could go where he wouldn't eventually find me.

I sat at the table.

CHAPTER 10

DAMN IT, JERRY

I tried to call Jerry after dinner, but the phone just rang. I waited a half hour, then called again, with the same result: the unending buzz of the Anderson family's phone ringing in my ear. I cradled the receiver—I was in the kitchen, in case I got Jerry on the line and needed some privacy—wondering where they might've gone. I was halfway to my room when a sneaky little thought wormed into my head—a Jerry thought, if ever I had one.

I went out into the living room where Mom and Dad sat on the sofa in front of the TV and looked out the open window—one of Dad's cross-breeze windows—facing Jerry's house. It was at least a half hour 'til sundown, maybe more, so I could clearly see Mr. Anderson's car in their driveway: it looked like they were home. I could also see Jerry's dad was trying to create a cross breeze of his own, and when I got right up to the screen, pressing one ear to it while plugging the other with a finger, I even heard faint voices from the direction of their open window. Someone was shouting about people being police officers, and I knew they were home: Jerry's dad never missed an episode of *Mod Squad* if he could help it.

I picked up the phone from its stand beside the couch, playing the wall cord out across the floor behind my parents. It was plugged into the wrong side of the room for me—toward Ray's house—so I only got it to the other end of the couch before I had to put it on the floor and dial the number.

"It's not enough that you're going to break the phone in the kitchen?" I looked up and saw my father glaring over the couch back. "You have to beat up this one too?"

I could tell he was still unhappy about the way I'd acted in the bathroom, so I kept my voice soft and calm. "I'm just checking on something. I'll be quiet, and I'll put it right back."

I finished dialing, then went to the window. This cord wasn't nearly as long as the one in the kitchen, though, and I had to hold the receiver in one hand and stretch my arm out to get my head back to the gap where I could hear. From the handset came the faint *buzz... buzz...* of the Anderson phone ringing again, but though I heard music with a fast beat and lots of horns—a chase scene, most likely—from their TV, there was no ringing at all from their open window. Damn it, Jerry.

I put the phone back on its stand and could tell from his stillness Dad might've been facing the television, but he was paying attention to me. Without a word I went into the kitchen but didn't turn down the hall toward my room. I was already in hot water, so there was no way this was going to go over well; taking a page from Jerry's book—the page titled, *Sometimes It's Easier to Apologize Later Than to Get Permission Now*—I slipped out the back door and ran up the side of the house to the street.

I rang the doorbell, shifting from foot to foot, forcing myself to calm down and stand still by the time Jerry's mom opened the door—though I couldn't help bursting out with "Hi, Mrs. Anderson, is Jerry home?" just as soon as I saw her face.

"Hi. What?—I mean, yes, but *Mod Squad*—"

"It's kind of important. I tried calling, but I think there's something wrong with your phone."

From behind her came Mr. Anderson's voice—it must have been a commercial. "There's nothing wrong with the phone; Jerry was on it earlier. Hey, wait a minute, there's no dial tone. I—oh! Here's the problem. The phone cord must've come loose in the socket—I've told that kid he's going to break the thing, the way he drags it around. There we go. All better. He'll have to be more careful."

Oh, he'd been careful, all right, unplugging the phone while making it look plugged in. "Good. Okay." I struggled to keep my voice calm. "So, since I'm here, can I talk to Jerry? Please?"

"Sure. He's in his room—been there for hours. He doesn't want to talk to us about it, but I think he's taking Ray awful hard." I was staring past her, toward Jerry's room, when she put a hand on my shoulder and a cool fingertip beneath my chin, tipping my face up so she could look full into it. Her own face was drawn into a slight frown. "How about you? I understand you got a real eyeful yesterday. Are you okay?"

I'd been so focused on Jerry the question took me by surprise, and without thinking I gave her a more truthful answer than I'd even given my parents.

"As long as I stay busy and don't think about it straight on, I'm okay. You know what I mean?"

Her face softened a little, and she stepped aside, inviting me into the house. "Well, he's in his room. You know the way."

"Thanks, Mrs. Anderson. Mr. Anderson."

She patted my back as I passed, while he just grunted; the commercial break was over. I went through the kitchen and down the hall, following the music seeping through one of the doors—Jerry and Ray's houses are built pretty much like mine, and we all have the smaller back bedrooms. I knocked but walked right in with barely a pause... and got that feeling—that thing with the weird French name, *vu-vu dey* or something like that—that I had done all this before. And I had: this was the second back bedroom I'd walked into today, trying to talk to Jerry, and this time I didn't even have to look around to know the room was empty.

Jerry was gone.

I'd suspected he was—worse, *known* he was gone but not wanted to believe it—as soon as I figured out he might have fudged the phone, but walking into that empty room was still a little like getting socked in the gut: all the breath went out of me and I felt like throwing up. I was standing there, wondering what to say to the Andersons— wondering if I should say *anything*, Jerry might be back before they noticed—when Mrs. Anderson was suddenly in the open doorway behind me, her footsteps covered by the sound of Styx's "Lady" coming from the radio on the desk and my own heart pounding in my ears.

"Would you boys like some... Jerry?" She looked around the room, then said his name again, glancing over her shoulder, checking the bathroom door I think; it was open, the room obviously empty. Then she looked at me. "Where's Jerry?"

This time his name sounded more fearful than curious, and I think she was putting things together in her mind: the long-playing radio, Jerry's silence, how upset he was. Jerry was smart, partly because he didn't come from stupid people. I hadn't had a chance to even try to come up with an answer when the question came again—this time lashing like a whip, any concern for me lost in the wave of worry about her own son. "Where's Jerry?"

I opened my mouth, but all I could do was stare at her. She took in my expression and her eyes grew hard, though still glittering with welling tears, before she turned away, shouting, "Harv! Jerry's gone! Harv—you turn that damn TV off now! *Jerry's gone!*"

"I don't know."

"You were talking to him earlier this evening," said my father. He sounded angry, but whether from my answer or just the whole situation, I couldn't tell.

"He didn't say anything about going anywhere," I said. "Honest, I don't know where he could be."

"But you knew something was wrong with our phone," said Mrs. Anderson. My father stood in front of me and she beside me, but while he hung back a bit she loomed close, sounding like she wanted to shake answers out of me—possibly only the presence of those same two cops was stopping her. "How did you know something was wrong with our phone?"

"Your car was in the driveway, but no one answered when I called—I just thought it was broken or something."

"But you talked to him," she shouted. "He didn't say anything? What the hell did you talk about for so long, then?"

I was crying again, wishing the cops would step in or something—she was right up to me, face-to-face—but they didn't move a muscle. "We were talking about Ray and Tommy," I burst out. "He was upset, and I was upset, and then Dad was banging on the door and scaring me, and he hung up while Dad was shouting from the hall, and I tried to call him back, but the line was busy—"

I'd run out of breath, but when I tried to pull in more air my chest hitched twice, hard, with a pair of hiccups that made me gag.

"That's enough."

My father just stared at the floor, where his gaze had gone while I tried to answer, but Mrs. Anderson, spun toward the new voice. "But—"

"I said, that's enough." Mom was using the tone that even my dad walked carefully around. She stepped between Jerry's mom and me, sliding one arm about my shaking shoulders. "I know you're upset, Brenda, but think about it. If he knew where Jerry was, why would he go over there looking for him?" She shook her head. "We have to use our heads. Officers?" All attention in the room shifted to the two men in uniform standing in what was becoming their customary spot in the doorway, Jerry's dad rooted between them.

"We have the picture you supplied," the older officer said to Jerry's mom. "They have it downtown right now, making copies and disseminating them to all the patrolmen, then forwarding it out to stations in the surrounding area. There's a Detective Howard on his way here right now to take charge of the investigation—with all that's been happening in this neighborhood recently, ma'am, we're taking this very seriously."

"I should hope so," said Mrs. Anderson, and her voice had become a cracked and broken thing I could barely hear, even though I still stood close beside her.

"And I'm sorry, son," said the cop, addressing me while he looked at Mom, "but that detective is going to want to talk to you when he gets here."

"Of course," Mom answered, her arm tightening around me.

"If you could come with me, ma'am," he said, holding out an arm to Mrs. Anderson. "Detective Howard is going to your house first. We should be there to greet him, don't you think?" Mrs. Anderson gave a spluttery nod and went to her husband, arms folded across her chest and shoulders shaking. Old cop and young cop glanced at each other, and old cop jerked his chin in our direction. Then he and the Andersons left to meet the detective, while young cop—who hadn't spoken a word since entering our house—stood beside our front door like some kind of guard.

"Come on." Mom's arm gently pushed me into motion, then guided me toward the couch, and we took a seat together. Dad came and stood awkwardly beside us, still looking at the floor.

"I'm... I'm sorry I scared you in the bathroom," he said. "It's just... so much is going on, and what you saw at the church yesterday, and... and I was just worried about you is all."

"S'okay," I said, a little stunned. Off the top of my head I couldn't think of any other time he'd apologized to me—and only once or twice to Mom. He seemed willing to accept my single word of forgiveness without a fuss, though, and gave me a brief double pat to one shoulder before striding off into the kitchen. We heard a sigh, the opening and closing of the refrigerator door, and the *pop-hiss* of an opening beer bottle, as Mom and I sat under the watchful gaze of the younger patrolman, waiting for our own visit from Detective Howard.

CHAPTER 11

THERE WAS NO RESPONSE

t was nearly ten o'clock before I stumbled into my room again, exhausted and lightheaded. Mom and Dad had sat on either side of me on the couch like bookends for the detective's visit. Detective Howard, tall, with dark hair and eyes and a nice suit—but also with a big fleshy nose and acne-pitted cheeks, nothing like the handsome detectives on TV—had sat in front of us in a chair he brought in from the kitchen. He'd asked questions, and I'd answered: no, I had no idea where Jerry was; we'd been talking about Ray, and what he was like, and how he might have wound up in front of that car; Jerry thought the newspaper reporter's speculation had been a load of crap, but I wasn't so sure; no, I had no idea where Jerry was. I'd stayed pretty calm and stuck to the truth—just avoided mentioning anything about Ray maybe being crazy, maybe being haunted, or maybe feeling guilty.

He'd been nice enough, but we went over it a few times, the same questions—sometimes with different words, but the same meanings—until I'd suddenly reached the end of my rope and started to droop. There hadn't been any warning—no yawning, eye blinking, or even feeling tired—I was just suddenly beat, and having trouble keeping my eyes open. Mom noticed right away and told the detective we were done, and he hadn't argued, just thanked us for our cooperation, asked me to let him know if Jerry tried to contact me, and was putting the kitchen chair back before Dad could do it for him.

Now I sat on my bed toeing off my sneakers, thinking about getting undressed. Deciding I was too wrung out to care about the clothes, I snapped off the bedside lamp and let my head hit the pillow. Everything from that night streamed through my mind: talking to Jerry, sneaking to his house, talking to the cops, everything. It was the kind of thing that would usually keep me awake, my brain running on overdrive and unable to turn off, but nothing was going to keep me from sleeping right then. My bedroom started to fall away—and there was a sound from my window.

I opened my eyes, pulse quickening, expecting to see Jerry's face hanging outside my screen as I had that afternoon. The words *Jesus, Jerry, do you know what I've been through* sprang to my lips... but got no farther; there was no face to be seen. "Jerry?" I whispered; there was no response.

It had been my imagination—I had been halfway to sleep. I closed my eyes again, wondering where Jerry might have gotten to, and if I would hear from him, and hoping he was all right. He'd sounded pretty far from all right on the phone, but—

There was a noise at the window again.

My eyes popped open. I hadn't been half asleep that time, and there was no way I'd imagined it; a brief, sharp slap. The open lower half of the window remained empty, however, with no silhouette or movement I could see. "Jerry?" I whispered.

Nothing.

I swung my feet to the floor and leaned closer, putting my head just a foot from the screen. From there I could see quite a bit of our yard, including the ground in front of the window where Jerry might stand if he couldn't keep his monkeylike grip on the sill. The yard was empty. But there had been a noise, I was sure of it. I'd been lying there with my eyes shut, but awake.

"Jerry?" In the quiet night, my hoarse stage-whisper might have carried all the way to the far side of the yard.

Nothing.

Holding my breath, listening for any sound, I leaned closer, trying to see the ground right below the window, thinking perhaps Jerry had fallen the three of four feet straight down and twisted his ank—

With a sharp flap, something was suddenly plastered to the other side of the screen, just two inches from my face. My held breath came out in an explosive "PUH!", all the air rushing out before my voice box could turn it into a scream. The edge of my bed took me out at the back of my knees as I launched myself away from the window, turning my flight for life into a clumsy backward sprawl. My head missed the mattress on the far side, snapping back so the bedframe whacked me a good one on the base of my skull. My lungs yanked in air to rectify the scream situation as I rebounded, the mattress acting like the weak trampoline I'd pretended it was when I was four or five. It threw me a few inches into the air, whipping my head forward, bringing the window back into view—and I clamped my lips against the scream as my body jounced to the sheet.

Outside the breeze died down, releasing the sheet of paper it had held against the screen and allowing it to fall away with a gentle flutter.

The planned scream oozed out between my teeth as a hiss as I sat up and yanked the screen open. I stuck my head out and the wind rose again, flipping up the note that had been taped to the sill, smacking me in the face with it this time. I jerked it loose, sat on the bed, and snapped my lamp on.

I get it now. I know why Ray was running. Ray was wrong about the deal. I wasn't a genius. I was an idiot. But I think I know what to do. Know where to go where he won't follow. Its so obvious I wish Ray had thought of it or asked me or something. Havent slept—wont leave me alone. Head kind of foggy but so OBVIOUS. Sorry I got you yelled at. You should go somewhere maybe he wont find you. You should go. Got to go.

It was a hurried scrawl, but it was Jerry's. He must've come by while I was at dinner and left the note when he found my room empty. I started for the door, thinking this was just the kind of thing Detective Howard was looking for—but stopped after a couple of strides.

The deal.

The only deal I could think of—especially one where Ray had called him a genius—was the one he'd struck with Tommy Taglioni: ride the wheel and be one of the gang, or chicken out and go home. He was right, he had been an idiot. We all had: not one of us had had any inkling it might backfire this badly. We were concerned about whether or not Tommy would ride the wheel, never thinking that if he did it could ruin all our lives. Offering that deal had been, without doubt, the stupidest thing Jerry'd ever done.

They might not be able to tell what the deal was from the note, but it was pretty obvious (OBVIOUS) that I knew about it, and they'd make me tell. I wasn't going to kid myself about that: they'd make me tell. And whether I wanted to tell or not, I knew Jerry didn't want me to. His whole reform school speech rose up in my head, then the way I'd failed Ray—failed to be a friend to my two best friends—and I knew I couldn't give the note to the police. Couldn't even give it to my parents.

I wasn't going to fail to be a friend this time.

I folded the note and slipped it under my pillow, quietly closed the screen, turned off the lamp and lay back down. I pulled the note out again, reading it slowly by the dim light spilling through my window, then refolded it and put it back. I was more than a little freaked out that Jerry thought Tommy was back and haunting him—had haunted Ray to his death—and I wanted more than anything to talk to him and find out what was going on, but that didn't seem likely. Not anymore. All I could do, I thought, was trust Jerry to know what he was doing. Jerry was smart. Jerry was wily. Jerry would figure things out—he always did. It was the last thought I had before sleep finally took me, sometime after midnight.

Jerry knows what he's doing.

They found Jerry the next morning at the base of the Ferris wheel. He'd landed on that little fence they used to keep the crowd away from the ride, and from what I overheard from a couple of the cops who came to our house, he must've been pretty high up when he fell: he'd landed on his back, and the fence had folded him in half.

The cops didn't know I overheard them—didn't even know I was there, in fact. They'd come around to poke about in the yard, probably looking for something very much like the note hidden under my pillow. I lay on my bed, listening. I couldn't see them from where I was, and they couldn't see me, but their quiet voices drifted in through the same half-open window that had let in both

Jerry and his note. I didn't think they were supposed to be back there, but Dad wasn't going to catch them snooping: he was in the living room, arguing with Detective Howard.

The detective had shown up right in the middle of breakfast, and when I saw his face I knew it wasn't going to be good. He'd brought the news that they'd found Jerry, and where, and wanting to question me about it. Mrs. Anderson had shown up practically on his heels, outraged at the news about Jerry and demanding answers from me—and trailing a uniformed officer like a small dog being forced to go out for a walk. The officer had looked absolutely miserable to be there, and it was obvious he didn't know how to stop her. Dad had immediately sent me to my room and the three men—the officer, the detective, and the dad—set to work getting Brenda Anderson to go back home. That was okay with me; I couldn't think of anything to say anyway.

So, I'd gone to my room and lain down, resting my head on top of the note I now understood better, wondering for a moment at the dryness of my eyes. I didn't feel sad enough to cry. I should have, I knew, but I felt like the time I'd had a cavity filled and Dr. Morris had used laughing gas on me: I knew I was awake, but I didn't *feel* awake, like none of this was really real, and I was just watching myself from the inside. *Funny*, I thought. I'd figured Mrs. Taglioni was going to eventually run out of tears—never occurred to me that the one doing that would be me.

"You questioned him last night!"

My father's voice punched through the haze I was in, rising from the relative quiet that had fallen after Mrs. Anderson left. It was the same tone he'd used on old cop and young cop when they'd shown up at our door for the first time, only louder. Maybe angrier.

"For two hours," he went on—definitely angrier. "He didn't know anything then, and he doesn't know anything now!"

"Sir," said Detective Howard, his volume up as well, though much calmer. "I just want to ask—"

"It's not his fault you didn't find Jerry—you wouldn't even have known Jerry was gone if he hadn't figured it out."

"And I appreciate that," said Howard. "But—"

"Shouldn't you be at the scene, Detective? Looking for clues?"

"I've been to the scene," said Howard, and he finally sounded annoyed. "Now I'm here. Asking about the death of his friend. One of his *best* friends, from what I understand, and the third one to die this week! Something's going on in this neighborhood, something that has to do with the kids. I'd think that as a parent you might actually want me to get to the bottom of it."

"I do... I just..." Dad was quieter now, not as sure of himself. "What about the carnival? All the trouble started when the carnival got to town, right? Doesn't it make sense that—"

"We are looking at the carnival," said Howard, quieter himself, but still firm. "The Ferris wheel's been shut down since the Taglioni kid, and as of this morning the whole thing is shut down. There are a whole bunch of unhappy carnies over there. But on this end of things, there's only the kids to look at, and your son is the last one on this street."

"But... he was the reason you were even called last night."

"And we appreciate that. And I understand that last night he claimed not to know anything—and he might not. But he might. He might know something he doesn't think is important, so he won't bring it to our attention. Something that won't come to the surface if no one's talking to him about it. This isn't some television drama, where I'm going to put him under the light and sweat it out of him; all I want to do is ask him some questions."

"But like you said, Detective," came my mother's voice. "Three of his best friends died this week—and he was having a hard time dealing with the first one. I'd rather you not talk to him until he's had a chance to rest and deal with the shock of it all."

"But ma'am," Detective Howard began.

"I'd rather you not," Mom said again, in the same tone she'd used when Mrs. Anderson was trying to bully me; she was being polite about it but was telling him no just as clearly as when Dad had told Jerry to stop calling. There was silence, long enough that I heard my heart go *thud-thud thud-thud*.

"I understand, ma'am," said the detective. Footsteps shuffled: Detective Howard was on his feet and leaving. "Here's my card. Let me know when he's ready to talk—but please, call me within the next day or so." His voice took on a tone that matched my mother's. "I can only *give* you the next day or so."

There were no words of goodbye, only the front door closing and he was gone. I lay there, still listening, but there was only the murmur of my parents' voices, far too quiet to catch their meaning. No longer distracted by their conversation, I was suddenly aware of the sensation of being watched from the window—though I may have caught a sound—and opened my eyes, which I hadn't realized until right then I'd even closed.

I expected to see a cop peeking in like Jerry had, though maybe not clinging to the side of the house like some cut-rate Spiderman. But I'd missed him, and the window was empty. I considered leaping to my feet and shouting, catching them in the act of peeping in my window and snooping in the backyard, but all they'd seen was me lying here looking asleep. I didn't see any harm in letting them keep thinking that, and maybe there would be some way to use it to my advantage later on: I imagined sitting in a courtroom witness box, like they did on *Perry Mason*, pointing at the two officers and saying "That's them. Those were the men poking around in our backyard—and that one even looked in my window!" Then I thought that I couldn't identify them if I never saw them. I slipped from my bed, staying low, and slunk the couple of feet to the window. I raised my head slowly, peeked out with one eye, and sighed. I shouldn't have bothered with all the stealth; the backyard was empty. I'd missed them.

I started out to the kitchen to grab the phone and drag the receiver into the bathroom: if there was a way to use the cops peeping in my window to my advantage, Jerry would know. Jerry always knew about stuff like—

It hit me like a punch, straight through my fog, that I couldn't call Jerry. That I'd never talk to Jerry again. Without warning I burst into tears, all the tears I thought I'd run out of. I crumbled onto the bed and cried longer than I thought possible, until my eyes swelled, my head ached, and my stomach hurt. I cried for Jerry, and I cried for Ray, and I even cried for Tommy again, though I'd been sure that particular well had run dry. I cried until the world around me stopped looking wavy and watery and started looking dim and dark; I thought for a moment I'd cried all day, and night was falling, but all I'd done was cry myself to sleep, and even as I realized it was happening I was already gone.

CHAPTER 12

I COULD'VE SWORN...

I woke with a start, snuffed some cry-snot into the back of my throat, choked, coughed it up into my mouth, reflexively gulped it down, then fought the wave of nausea brought on by the cold, disgusting, swallowing-a-clam-whole feel of the gunk as it slid down my gullet. I breathed in and out, hard and fast, blinking my gummy eyes until I'd managed to convince my stomach to stay down where it belonged. I looked around my room, as confused as I always was when I took a daytime nap.

I checked my bedside clock, and though I wasn't certain what time I'd actually fallen asleep, I thought I'd only slept for a half hour or so. Could that be right? I looked around the room again, wondering what had woken me out of what had felt like a sound sleep, and my eyes went to the half-open window.

The window. Somebody had been watching me from the window, I was sure of it. Had those two cops come sneaking back, peeking in to keep an eye on me? Not wanting to be too slow again, I tried to leap to my feet, but I was still so out of it all I managed was an awkward, tangled half-fall to the window, catching the sill for balance.

Nothing. The yard was empty again.

I must have woken up slower than I thought. Or maybe I imagined they were there. Remembered them looking in earlier and just dreamed it?

A sound behind me; a sense of motion. Mom, I thought, hearing my clumsy movement again and opening the door to see if I was all right. I turned—and found the door still closed, no sign of a worried parent anywhere.

That's weird, I thought. *I could've sworn...*

The breeze from the open window touched the back of my neck, and there was something—a sound? I couldn't be sure—on that breeze, and I knew there was someone out there. I spun back, sneaky cops on my mind, thinking they must be watching, but if they were, then it was like when they kept people under surveillance in the movies: they were trying to see without being seen, from a parked car or the back of a van somewhere.

This was my own backyard, though, and there was no place to hide out there I hadn't already found during hundreds of games of hide-and-seek with the guys. I'd been littler then—hide-and-seek wasn't the coolest thing to play once you hit eleven—but it hadn't been all that long ago, and I still remembered all the really good places. As I scanned the yard, though, I saw that all the really good places were good for a ten-year-old. Grownups wouldn't have fit under any of the bushes, or behind the birdbath.

My eyes went to the top of the fence, racing along its upper edge, looking for any hint of movement from the other side where Mrs. Boardman's yard, over on Baker Street, backed up against our own.

They might have talked Mrs. Boardman into letting them watch our house from over on her property. I'd seen them do that on TV. Or I could just be paranoid, and all I heard was Mrs. Boardman hanging her washing on the line or someth—

"You okay in here?"

With a shout I whirled to find the door open this time, Mom half in and half out, hand still on the knob, concern plastered all over her face.

"What?" I said—I'd been so focused on the back fence and neighbor's yard, it was the only response that would come.

"I heard a thud," she said. "It was so quiet in here for so long I started to get worried, and then that thud..." She came around the bed to stand with me at the window and put a soft hand to the side of my face.

"Are you doing all right?" Her voice was gentle again, but I wasn't sure what to say. I'd been numb, cried myself to sleep, and now I was apparently paranoid about the old woman in the house behind us being in cahoots with the cops. I wondered for an instant if I was in some bizarre dream, but Mom was still standing there, palm to my cheek, waiting for an answer. The breeze stirred her dark hair around the edges of her face.

"Sort of?" I said.

"You don't sound very sure of yourself."

"I'm not, really."

She dropped her hand and moved out from behind the bed, but stopped in the doorway again, turning to face me as she had when she'd entered: half in, half out, hand on the doorknob, though this time her face was blank. "You know... you can come talk to us about anything. Anything at all. Anything you're dealing with or... or into. Okay? We're here for you."

"I know," I said, a little bewildered.

"We're here for you," she repeated, backing out and pulling the door quietly closed.

Well that was weird, I thought. *Whatever I'm "dealing with" or "into"? What does she think I'm—*

"Son of a bitch," I whispered.

I'd been so busy worrying about Jerry, and feeling terrible about everything in general, I'd forgotten to worry what this might look like to anyone who knew even less about it than me. There had been four boys living on this street, three of them best friends, and it was like the detective had said: now there was one. Me. He wanted to question me, thinking I knew something, and Mom wanted to protect me—was trying hard to give me the benefit of the doubt—but she was wondering if I knew something, too. Jerry had gone out through a back window, and the next time anybody saw him, he was dead. I wasn't sure if they had figured out how Tommy'd gotten out of his house that night, but for all I knew he'd gone out the back window, too. He'd gotten over that carnival fence somehow, hadn't he? But they might not know about that; all they knew was he'd gotten out somehow—or someone had taken him, maybe—and he'd wound up dead by dawn.

Was that why the cops had been in our backyard? They suspected that I knew something—were they worried I might pull a disappearing act too, only to be found somewhere when the sun came up, maybe at the base of the tallest ride at the carnival? It made a weird sort of sense when I tried to think about it from their point of view—and actually, they were right. I *did* know something, though even I didn't know what to make of it.

And what was I thinking? Jerry'd thought Ray was crazy for a while—seeing things, hearing voices, whatever—been just as cynical as always, but eventually... eventually he'd believed. In the end he'd believed with everything he had. They both had. And what had they believed? My mind tried to turn away from it, instinctively understanding that to recognize it was just a step on the road toward believing it myself, but...

I don't think Ray was nuts.

They'd believed Tommy was back and following them again. But they both said they'd never seen or heard him—Jerry'd even wished he *could*—and that made no sense to me. I—

The back of my neck crawled with a sensation that had nothing to do with the breeze. I spun to the window, aware that someone was watching me, and wanting to catch them. I scanned the hiding places and fence line again, putting my hands on the sill and really looking, thinking that I'd still not seen Mrs. Boardman, or her laundry, and that if I could just catch one of the cops in the act...

I saw nothing; no hint of motion, nor anything that might not have belonged. But I could've sworn there had been someone—

I froze, with a sudden hollow, sick feeling in my belly. Someone had been there, behind me, I'd felt them watching... someone I couldn't see. There was no one there, but there was.

You don't get to see him, Jerry had said, while wishing he was crazy, because crazy can be cured. *He's just there, and you know it, and there ain't a thing you can do about it.*

I'd thought someone was in the yard, but no one was there. I'd thought Mom was in the doorway, but she hadn't gotten there yet. How many times over the past couple of days had I gotten up to look for someone, or turned expecting to see someone, only to find no one there? Was Tommy tagging along again, always behind and trying to catch up? Was he, even now—

My spine went wild with the creepy-crawlies, and he was behind me, I knew he was behind me. I spun to face the empty room—but that put my back to the window, and there was just so much space out there, so many places for him to be. I took two steps sideways, out from in front of the window, but there was still air behind me. I threw myself backward the eight or ten inches to the wall and my shoulders hit with an impact that shook the house.

He'd pulled a kitchen chair into his room and he was sitting there with his back to the wall, Jerry had said about Ray, *but he was still looking over his shoulder, like he was expecting someone to be there.* And I might've been just freaking out because of what Jerry'd said, but someone was still there, according to the feeling I had in my back and shoulders, the weird, skin-crinkling feeling of being watched, though that was impossible, there couldn't be anyone there—

And then there *was* someone there. My bedroom door flew open, Dad framed in the doorway with Mom looking, wide eyed, over his shoulder.

"What the hell was that?" shouted my father, sounding half angry, half afraid. He took a step into the room, prodded, I think, by my mother, who stepped in beside him, looking at me with mixed suspicion and concern. I stared back without speaking for a second or two, just happy to have someone else in the room with me, my heart still racing from everything I'd figured out just moments ago.

"Well?"

"I, uh, slipped?" I tried. "Tripped over my own feet and fell into the wall. Sorry about that." He was still looking at me, and I started babbling. "You know how you're always telling me to be more careful, pay more attention, stuff like that. I guess you were right, I need to be more careful. Sorry. I didn't mean it. Sorry."

He held up a hand like it could slow the flow of my words. "It's okay. I was just—we were—"

"We were just worried about you," Mom supplied. "The noise and all, we thought you might be hurt. Just try to be more careful." She touched Dad's forearm, and they started to turn... and I realized they were about to leave me alone again. But would I really *be* alone?

I shoved myself off the wall and stepped right up onto my bed, something Mom would have spoken to me about if the situation were different. I thudded to the floor on their side of the room and my father jerked in surprise— I'd moved so fast I'd startled him.

"I'm kind of tired of my room. You mind if I come out there and be with you guys for a while?"

I was still talking way too fast, like I'd never stopped babbling, and Dad just blinked and turned to Mom.

"Of course not," Mom said. "You're not punished or anything—we just thought you wanted to be in your room." She put a hand on Dad's shoulder. "You can watch TV with your father while I fix us some lunch. I think *Let's Make A Deal* is coming on."

Dad turned without a word, and Mom followed him out toward the living room. I brought up the rear, crowding Mom's heels a bit, repeating silently to myself like a mantra, *That was all in your head... that was all in your head...* The whole walk down the hall I was fighting not to look over my shoulder to check and see if we were being followed. I didn't need to look: I was more than just afraid Tommy was there.

I could feel him.

CHAPTER 13
TODAY'S TUESDAY

We watched *Let's Make A Deal*, eating tuna sandwiches and chips from TV trays. Dad sat in his easy chair while I perched on the couch, repeating my mantra and trying not to twist around and scan the room every thirty seconds. Even though I was determined to act normal, I was far too fidgety to pay any real attention to what we were watching. Dad even barked, "Will you settle down?" a couple of times. But I wasn't watching the screen: I was too busy thinking.

It's all in my head. After Jerry's story, and then that note, who wouldn't be jumping at shadows? Jerry was right, right? Me and Ray, gullible to the end, just like he said—mass hypnosis, like he claimed that spoon guy used. Spooky stuff doesn't happen in the daylight, anyway. *This is all because it's on my mind. All I have to do is think about something else for a while.*

By the end of *Deal* I knew that it was all in my mind, and all I had to do was not think about it for long enough, and the sensation of being watched would just go away. *$10,000 Pyramid* came on, and I settled down to pay attention to the show... but it was just like any other time I tried not to think about something: the harder I tried not to think about it, the more I thought about it. I still had no idea what was happening on the small screen in front of us, but I did manage, through sheer force of will, not to look around anymore.

Then, on the commercial break, Dad went to the bathroom. The feeling of being watched magnified like an itch I couldn't scratch. I knew no one was there—I broke down and checked—but once I set my mind to rigidly staring at the TV again it changed. For an instant it felt like someone were about to tap me on the shoulder, like I'd just caught a flash of their hand from the corner of my eye. I looked, then looked again. I was scared, and concentrating so hard on not looking *again*, I didn't hear Dad coming back until he plopped down into his chair beside me, and I uttered a little yelp. With Dad back it got a little better—I was *supposed* to feel like someone was in the room with me then, he was sitting right there—but I still had no idea what was happening on the show.

After Pyramid, Dad had some things to do out in the yard. He looked surprised when I offered to help, but it was that or try to follow Mom around the house. I needed something to distract me, and right then there was no way I wanted to be left alone, even if it meant going out and weeding the lawn. So, I spent some time pulling dandelions while Dad pruned the bushes along the front of the house. I did so much of the work my father even pulled out the lawn mower, saying that, what with all that had been going on this week, he'd missed his regular Saturday grass-cutting, and now it was just growing wild—though to be honest, I couldn't see a big difference.

His saying he'd missed his Saturday cut made me do a little math; I was never good at keeping track of what day it was when school was out, and he was right, there had been a lot going on lately. The carnival had opened on Wednesday; I remembered that much. I did a little counting on my fingers, tallying up the days since I'd last heard that wheezing little *Wait up, guys*, and let out a small "huh" when I realized I really had lost track of the days. I looked over at Dad, who was checking the oil level in his well-used power mower.

"Hey Dad?"

"Yesss?" he said, drawing the word out as he tilted his head sideways to check the line on the dipstick.

"Today's Tuesday."

"Yesss?" he said again, wiping the stick clean before plunging it back in and screwing it down, apparently satisfied.

"What're you doing home?" I said, for it occurred to me that while my father and I had just watched television together in the middle of the day, it was a day he should've spent in the office, a place he'd gone every weekday— except for holidays and one vacation week a year—for as long as I could remember. He'd even gone in once with the flu, so sick his coworkers had forced him to come home halfway through the day for their own safety, afraid of an office-wide epidemic.

He crouched over the machine for a moment, even though the dipstick had been replaced and he wasn't doing anything to the mower that I could see, hunkered at the edge of the walkway with his back to me. "I... well... your mother... yes, your mother was worried, what with the police being here to talk to you this morning."

His words gained speed as he finally rose to his feet, wiping his hands on the dipstick rag and turning to face me. "She was quite worried. Still is. Oh, she's covering it up some—doesn't want to upset you, you understand—but she asked me to stay home to help her out, keep her company, that sort of thing. So, I had to stay home. For your mother."

He tucked the rag into his back pocket, lowering his chin a bit to peer at me from beneath his brow.

"Look, son, I know you've been through a lot, and it's not your fault; I understand that. But your mom is really concerned about you. She doesn't know what's going on, and it's frightening her. So, if there's anything you can tell say—anything at all—that would help ease her mind, I'd take it as a bit of a favor if you could just tell her. It'd sure make my life a little easier right now if you could stop worrying her like this."

I thought of him pulling me out of the lake and shouting at me not to scare my mother before he walked away to finish crying. Remembered him coming to my room the other day, so obviously worried but unable to say so. Recalled that just a couple of hours earlier he'd been the one to burst into my room to see if I was okay—Mom had needed to poke him aside just to get in the door.

I almost told him right then. I'd wrestled with telling *someone* about what had happened at the carnival that night, and the only thing that had kept me from spilling the beans was Jerry's insistence that I wasn't in it alone, that anything I might say or do would have consequences for all of us, not just me—but there wasn't an *all of us* anymore, was there? That was why everyone wanted to talk to me, right? I was the only one left.

I'd dreamt of those hands gripping the safety bar as the Ferris wheel carried them up into the night. That had been the start of everything, before anyone had died, and if I could've taken it all back I would've. In a heartbeat. But that was the story everyone wanted to hear, and I was the only one who could tell it now.

I told him he'd be fine.

I looked at my dad, home from work to look after me, no matter what he said, opened my mouth to tell him, to just let it all spill out, even though it'd hurt him to hear what I'd done—and froze when his eyes shifted to look over my shoulder and he stiffened. I suddenly felt Tommy's presence behind me, and I almost burst into tears when I realized it had worked: I'd distracted myself and not felt a thing until this reminder. Now, though the feeling was back, and—

"*There* you are you little son of a bitch!"

I whirled, and rather than Tommy lurking behind me, Mrs. Anderson was storming across her lawn toward us, barefoot, hair in disarray, eyes shining with tears and strangely small without their usual coating of makeup. I just had time to feel a weird mix of relief, confusion, and then new fear before Dad's hand landed on my shoulder. She reached the flower bed bordering her property, bare feet crushing phlox as she marched straight across, shouting, "What did he say to you? What did he say?"

"Go in the house now," Dad said, giving me a tug. "And stay away from the windows. I'll see if I can get her calmed down—or at least back in her own house."

She stumbled in the soft earth of the flower bed, windmilling her arms for balance as I turned away. "Don't you go! Don't you go anywhere!"

"Brenda, please." Dad moved to intercept her. The front door opened as I hustled toward the house, and Mom stepped out, drawn by the commotion. Looking past her, I saw the side of Ray's house. A curtain twitched. Ray's mother stood in the window, holding the drapes aside to look out, watching the scene without making a move to get involved.

Mom came down the steps and went right past me, and I stopped for a moment, watching her go to help Dad with Jerry's mom. Mr. Anderson had come out of their house as well, but whether he was coming to try to calm his

wife or help her storm our house, I had no idea. A sound
from across the street drew my attention. The front door
of the Taglioni residence had opened, and Mrs. Taglioni
was motoring down their steps, chunky little legs churning
beneath her skirt hem. As angry as Jerry's mom looked,
Tommy's mom still looked only sad, and a sudden fear
gripped me that she wasn't on her way to help out with
Mrs. Anderson, but to hug me again, weeping, telling me
what a wonderful boy I was.

The thought of the one mother in the neighborhood
who should've been furious with me coming to my defense
goaded me into motion, and I fled into the house. I paused
for a second to look out at the scene—Mr. Anderson
arriving behind Mrs. Anderson, still standing in her
flowerbed, waving her arms and shouting at my parents as
Mrs. Taglioni approached in a sad-eyed flanking
maneuver—before I took my father's advice and got away
from the windows. I went straight back to my bedroom,
firmly closing the window to block out as much of the noise
as I could and then spinning back to the door as I realized
someone had followed me back and was standing right
behind—

But no one was there, of course. No one I could see.

I plunked down on my bed, wrapping my head with
my arms, trying to drown out the sounds of people arguing
that managed to seep in despite the closed room, but it
didn't work. Suddenly, all the little alarm bells went off in
my head that someone was close, *too* close, inside my
personal space—like when Ray would crowd in, so I could
feel him breathing on the back of my head. I backed away,
rolling off the bed toward the door, coming to my feet...

Nothing. The sensation ebbed slightly, as if he'd
stayed across the room rather than clinging right to me.
Tears came to my eyes when I remembered how I'd gotten

away from the feeling, distracted myself with my father, but now there was nothing to distract me, and the feeling (*Tommy*, part of my mind said, *it's Tommy*) was back, even stronger than before. I snatched *Stranger in a Strange Land* from my bookcase and lay down, hoping to lose myself in the story of Valentine Michael Smith, but I couldn't focus on the page. I read the first paragraph again and again, until I threw the book across the room in frustration. I wrapped my head in my arms again, tried to think of something else, anything else, but it was no use; all I could think was that he was still there.

He was still there.

CHAPTER 14

THIS WAS REAL

I looked at the bedside clock: 2:01 a.m.

I nearly cried.

Exhaustion, both mental and physical, was beating me down, and despair—the same despair I'd found so frightening in Jerry's voice during our last phone conversation—was crowding out all my thoughts. I hated the idea of being alone, but I was so tired and worn-out I just wanted to get some sleep. *Needed* to get some sleep. But all that would come to me as I lay there, dazed but awake, feeling him behind me—his weight on the mattress, his breath on the back of my neck, shuddering at the constant anticipation of his touch—were snippets of other people's words, words I'd picked up over the past few days.

Jerry: *They're gonna grab us, guilty or not. That'll mean jail. You want to go to jail, for something we can't fix anyway?*

Detective Howard: *I can only give you the next day or so.*

Jerry: *Being alone was bad. Worse than I thought.*

Even the note under my pillow: *Havent slept—wont leave me alone.*

My God, now I understood what he meant...

...The sun was hot, and the car ride had been long. Mom's voice chased me down the hill toward the short floating dock, but I wasn't listening: I was yanking my T-

shirt over my head and throwing it aside as I ran. I slowed but never stopped, toeing my sneakers loose and kicking them off before I got to the wooden planks. Dad's voice came then, but I was laughing, and couldn't make out his words either. I only had eyes for the beautiful, cool water that was going to feel so good against my overheated skin.

A small rowboat was tied to one side of the dock, an aluminum canoe to the other, clunk-clunking hollowly against the wooden slip in the small waves. I had no choice but to run to the very end of the platform before leaping high into the air, tucking my knees to my chest and wrapping them with my arms. I whooped and fell, fully intending to empty the lake with my perfectly executed cannonball.

I locked my teeth in a fierce grin as my butt hit the water with a painful slap, holding my breath as the water parted, allowing me to slip—with a truly massive splash, I was sure—down into the dark.

The shock hit, stealing away my thoughts. Cold— not the bone-numbing cold I'd read about in White Fang *and* Swords and Deviltry, *but something so frigid my confused skin felt it as painful heat—enveloped me. The sting to my backside disappeared into this body-wide insult. All my muscles jerked, parts pulling against parts in a kind of physical confusion, back straightening, legs twisting, arms flailing, stomach fluttering.*

I gasped.

Icy fire poured down my throat, splitting into twin rivers attacking my lungs, the freezing pain like a living thing trying to claw its way through my chest. Those lungs tried to fight off the invasion the only way they knew: they coughed. I choked. The overload to my skin began to fade—still feeling the pain, but now as cold, cold,

cold—but my lungs found no relief as they pulled. My arms and legs still flailed, I knew, but I didn't care about them; my whole focus centered around my lungs, trying to do their one simple job and breathe.

They failed.

Hands thrust through the black water, fingers spread to grab. I recalled where I was, that my father was there to drag me, kicking and puking, up and out of this frigid world of death and throw me, roughly, onto that sun-warmed dock. He would get the water out of me, the air into me, then hug, cry, and scold, but he was there. I reached, knowing all I had to do was take those hands and everything would be all right. Everything will be all—

The hands closed, grabbing something I hadn't seen before in the dark water. Just inches from my own, those fingers gripped a horizontal bar that lifted them up and away as they squeezed with white-knuckled intensity. I reached, tried to lunge after them, but the water gave me nothing to push against. I tried to scream, but all I managed was a weak bubbly sound—a sound that grew after I'd stopped making it. From bubbles to a fast heartbeat, then a rapid drumroll, rolling out faster and deeper as those hands—no longer my father's, but smaller, pudgier—clung to the bar carrying them up, away from me, into the night sky.

Soundless white fireworks burst at the edges of my fading vision as my lungs worked but nothing happened. The fireworks spread, filling the space above me with millions of points of light, and I realized that was the night sky up there, and not water around me, but air, and all I had to do was take a breath—just a single breath. But my frozen, battered lungs wouldn't do the job, couldn't do the job. I focused on the drumroll roar of the Ferris wheel engine, blasting its noise into the night. I was dying, but

all I could do was lie curled on the filth of that gondola
floor and let that traitorous, hateful, terrifying engine roll
me over the top and down the back side of the ride, down
to where there was safety and medicine and air and—
The roaring motor went suddenly silent.

I lunged awake, crying, gasping, and choking. My fist
thudded against my chest—once, twice—before I realized I
was breathing, fine and fast and hard, the lungs I thought
were frozen working like panicked bellows. Someone
crowded in behind me, not touching me but close, so close.
Feeling claustrophobic, wanting nothing in the world more
than space and air to—just to breathe—I scrambled
forward, off the bed, rolling to my feet and backing toward
the door, one hand sticking out to ward off...

No one.

I collapsed to my knees, not falling but folding up
like a piece of paper as fear-fueled strength drained out of
me, still crying, still gasping. I pulled in a shuddering
breath as my defensive arm drooped, dropping my hand to
the floor. "Tommy," I said, then had to pull in another
breath to continue. "Tommy, please... please, just leave me
alone."

It was the first time I'd spoken to whatever was
following me. I hadn't before, maybe out of stubbornness,
maybe out of some superstitious fear that saying anything
out loud about it would make it real; but I couldn't try to
ignore it anymore, couldn't tell myself that Ray and then
Jerry had just been hysterical, and a little over the edge.

This was real. It was all real.

According to my bedside clock, it was 2:07 a.m.; I'd
managed to have all that dream in just five minutes or so
of actual sleep, and still, Tommy was there. I knelt on the
rug, chest heaving, desperately trying to think of a way to

get rid of him, but again all I could think of were things people had said, stuff Jerry'd put in that note—.

The note. I lunged to my feet and took one full stride toward the bed and half of another before I stopped, pulling my reaching hand back from the sheets. I didn't want to invade the air above that mattress, afraid of what I might find lurking there. Waiting for me. I didn't see anything, sure, and my eyes were plenty used to the dark by then, and could clearly see the rumpled sheets and pillowcase, but the sense of him crowding behind me on that bed had been so *strong.* How could he not be there, watching me, waiting, until my reaching fingers came to rest against his shoulder, or chest, or—God help me—his *face*, smooth and fat and as naked as when he went into the ground?

With that thought, the shadows became too much for me, night-adapted eyes or not, and my reaching hand shot sideways. My bedside lamp came on with a click, its familiar glow chasing back the dark. There was nothing on my bed—I knew that even before turning on the lamp—but I still gritted my teeth and held my breath, very much as I had when leaping into the lake in my dream, as I forced myself to sit on the mattress and shove a hand beneath the pillow.

The note.

I didn't need to read it again: I'd read it so often I knew the thing by heart. But that didn't stop me from unfolding it and smoothing the battered sheet of notebook paper across my lap to look at it one more time.

I know why Ray was running.

Now I did, too: trying to get away from Tommy Tagalong, just like we always did. And Tommy was the one kid in the neighborhood Ray could have outrun. But could he? Could he really? How can you outrun someone who's not really there? How would you know if you even had?

Someone was reading over my shoulder. I felt them so close to me; their chest almost against my back, their face hovering beside mine, practically cheek-to-cheek.

A puff of breath kissed the side of my face, and it was cold.

It was *dank*.

I was up and off the bed, spinning to back toward the door again—oh, I knew why Ray had been running, Christ, how could he not—but my eyes shot back to the page in front of me, seeking out the words I had pulled it out specifically to read.

Havent slept—wont leave me alone.

He wouldn't. He wouldn't leave me alone. I understood it now, what I'd thought I'd understood when I found the damn note: why Jerry had gone to the Ferris wheel. *I think I know what to do. Know where to go where he won't follow.* Even when I hadn't believed Tommy was really back, that part had made sense to me: Jerry might've been a little crazy, but he wanted to get away from good old Tommy Tagalong, so he'd go to the one place he knew Tommy was afraid of—the one place he'd bank on Tommy not following. But he'd been foggy from not sleeping, panicked, not thinking clearly. He'd seen that he was wrong—hell, we'd all seen it. I was still seeing it, in my dreams: those clutching hands rising up into the night sky as the Ferris wheel engine sputtered and roared.

Tommy had gone up there, frightened or not. He'd shown up at the carnival and ridden the ride, then just followed Jerry back up there the other night. Had Jerry slipped? Had he been pushed? No, I didn't think so. I didn't think Tommy was back to punish us, like some fat, wheezy revenant from the comics, out for the blood of those who'd wronged him.

It was the deal.

I hadn't gotten it when I read the note that first time. I hadn't understood. *Ray was wrong about the deal I wasn't a genius. I was an idiot.* I'd thought Jerry was cursing the deal because it was how we'd all gotten into this thing, admitting that it was his brilliant plan that had gotten Tommy killed in the first place. Oh, we'd all had parts in it, but it had been his idea.

Now I understood that was only part of it—and the smaller part. Sure, the deal had gotten us all into this thing, but it was also why we were still in it. I'd seen it again and again in my dreams, seen it so often I wasn't seeing it for what it was anymore. But the new dream, the nightmare where I didn't just watch but *rode* the ride, pretty well drove it home for me:

We'd made a deal with Tommy Taglioni, and he'd gone through with it. Jerry hadn't thought he would in a million years, but he had, and now he was taking his spoils and enjoying what he'd won. *How would you like to just hang with us, no more having to chase us or anything, you know, as one of the gang?* Jerry had said, and that was what Tommy was doing now. Not chasing after us, or watching from a distance, but hanging with us, up close and personal. The kid I'd once thought of as *Tommy Taglilonely* had killed himself to have some friends—and now that he had us, he wasn't letting go.

But he didn't have friends now, did he? Not anymore. Now there was just me, and from the look of things he was determined never to be alone again. He was going to follow behind me, waiting for us to be alone, just the two musketeers, and then he'd munty right on up to me, and read over my shoulder, and sleep in my bed...

And Detective Howard was coming to take me in for questioning. He wasn't going to let it go—he *couldn't*, what with Jerry's mom after him to find out what I knew. And he *would* find out. I still had no illusions about that. He'd find out about the note, then he'd find out about the deal, and then he'd find out about my part in it—and what was it Jerry had said, way back a million years ago when we were standing in his yard?

Whatever we did or didn't do, if you go talking to someone about it, they're gonna grab us, guilty or not. That'll mean jail. You want to go to jail, for something we can't fix anyway?

Three kids dead. A mother demanding justice at the top of her voice—and that was before anyone knew what had really happened at the wheel. Ray was right: there was no way someone wasn't going to jail for this... and I was the only one left. Was I ready to go to jail for something we couldn't fix?

I thought about my dad, standing between me and the two cops, then between me and the detective, insisting that I didn't know anything. Taking my word for it that I didn't know anything. I thought of Mom, putting the detective off, demanding that he leave me alone, on my side even though she had doubts. I even thought of Mrs. Taglioni, convinced that I was Tommy's greatest friend after months of lies from her own son's mouth, and I wondered if she'd run out of tears yet.

It was going to let so many people down when it came out. *I* was going to let them down. But I couldn't see any way around it. All I could see at that moment was days, and then weeks, and then months—maybe years—living in a small cell, all alone except for my new best friend.

He'd come closer as the day went on, the more time we spent together. Nearer. I'd done everything now but hear the sound of his voice and feel the touch of his hand. But the breath on my cheek had been cold. Damp. A little earthy. What was he like, this kid I couldn't see? Was he still in the suit I'd seen him in, with its shiny buttons, and nicely knotted tie jammed tight beneath his thick, bullfrog throat? If I could see him, would his face still have that strange tan and healthy look, as if dying had actually be the best thing for the sickly boy? Or...

Or was it like stories I'd read in those comics Mom hated, *Creepy*, or *Eerie*, where the ghost didn't look like a living person, but looked the way they did in the grave? Was I going to share a cell with this specter, feeling him decay beside me? *Smelling* him?

"No," I whispered. "I'll go crazy pretty quick, I think, and wind up in a rubber room."

The sensation came again, a head hanging beside my ear, someone reading over my shoulder. Lost in thoughts of jail cells and funny farms, I reflexively turned toward the nosy parker—and that breath came again, an exhalation chill and damp, but this time against my lips and nose. I'd been inhaling when it came, and my nose and lungs filled with an icy blast of moist stink, like my own breath when I had a terrible cold, all steamy mucus and hot snot, but this was cold as the grave.

I gagged and staggered, clapping a hand over my mouth as my stomach leapt into my throat. I breathed hard, forcing air in and out, trying to rinse out all that nasty as I threw the note onto my desk; if he wanted to read it that bad, let him read it over there. I sat on my bed, arms crossed in front of my lowered head to try to hold him at bay as I caught my breath and tried not to vomit at the thought of what had just been inside me.

I can't do this, I thought. *I can't go on like this*. The thought of hours and days spent in Tagalong's company was terrifying. It had been less than a night, but I had to get out of there, had to get away from him—and I had to do it before Howard came to get me and I couldn't run any more. I got up and moved toward the door again; *If I stay moving,* I thought, *he can't get close.*

I looked at the note lying on the desk, but I didn't dare pick it up: he seemed to be attracted to it. I didn't need to see it anyway; I knew what it said, and I knew what Jerry had thought and I knew where he'd gone wrong.

At least, I *thought* I knew.

He'd been right: the deal had turned out to be the stupidest thing he'd ever done—that any of us had done—but there might be a way out of it. There *might.* Jerry had said he could hang with us, not chase after us anymore, and that was what Tagalong was doing. But what if, like Jerry'd said, I could get to a place where he wouldn't follow? Where he refused to hang with me? Wouldn't that break the deal?

Jerry had thought he knew where to go where Tommy wouldn't follow. But he'd been tired, and foggy, and wrong—he'd gone someplace Tommy might not *want* to go but knew he *could.* I thought I knew a place—a better place—where Tommy didn't know. Couldn't. But I'd have to go tonight—have to go now—because Detective Howard might show up at breakfast, as he had already, and then I'd be finished.

I started quietly opening drawers and pulling out clothes.

CHAPTER 15

WE SHOULD'VE LET YOU FLATTEN THE LITTLE CREEP

I t was almost three o'clock in the morning, and there wasn't a car in sight—nothing to slow down for as I hit the end of Tremont and took a left onto Main. I rode in a wide arc, still pedaling, still picking up speed—until I realized just what I was about to run over, locked up my rear wheel, and had to whip around sideways, leaning against the skid to keep from flipping over and leaving a patch of skin on the asphalt. Enough of that had happened here to last me a lifetime.

It was the spot where Ray died, broken and twisted, the day of Tagalong's funeral. The blood, if there had been any, had been washed from the street, but the skid marks were still there, thick and black under the streetlights, from where Ronald Burgess had jammed on his own brakes, trying to bring a ton and a half of Detroit steel to a stop and save a kid's life. I wouldn't have needed the skid marks to recognize it, though: the spot was burned into my brain.

I stared at the place Ray'd come to rest, his eyes open and staring, and I felt like I should say something. I had no idea what, but I hadn't said anything at all the day of the accident, just took off running too fast to stop. I felt the first little hairs rising at the back of my neck, telling me that, fast as I'd been riding, Tagalong was never far behind. I thought of that last day we'd all been together as friends—not the paranoid group that had met in Jerry's yard, one of us worrying about reform school and jail, another jumping at shadows he knew were no longer empty, but the three of us heading out for the first day of the carnival. I thought of us running from Tagalong that last time and the words came. They may not have been the best words, but they were the right ones for Ray.

"We should've let you flatten the little creep."

I wheeled my bike to the sidewalk, no more willing to roll over that spot than I'd be to just tromp on a grave in the churchyard. The hairs on the back of my neck were standing up high now, and the sense of being watched was almost unbearable. I wondered for a moment if traffic would've helped, if passing cars—and the people in them—would've been enough to keep Tagalong at least at an arm's length. If this worked, I'd never find out about that. If this worked, I'd never have to worry about it again.

If this worked.

I swung a leg over my Huffy and stood on the pedals, pumping hard, trying to leave Tommy behind. If only it would be that simple.

I had a shorter distance to go than when we'd all hiked out to the carnival—about a mile and a half, tops—and for most of it I felt alone, gloriously alone. Whenever I slowed down, though, either going uphill or out of breath, I'd get the feeling I was being followed. Not up close, and of course I never saw anything, and I may have been imagining it: my father likes to say we see what we want to see, when we look hard enough—and he doesn't mean it in a good way.

I kept a pace I never could've during the day, with its people, traffic, and sun beating down. I flashed past parked cars and dark houses, and though I'd been out at night before, it had always been with the guys. Alone, in the dark, the cars and houses looked spooky and abandoned, like in that Vincent Price movie, *The Last Man on Earth*. I nearly drove into one of those parked cars when a yard I was passing exploded with sound as a dog, probably startled to see a kid pedaling his bike like a madman in the middle of the night, went crazy barking. I let out a little scream, then a slightly hysterical laugh, pedaling faster as the pooch yowled behind me.

I didn't bother with the bike chain and lock when I got where I was going, just slung a leg high and hopping off the bike while it was still moving, giving the handlebars a little push. It free-rolled into the bushes by the fence, but I didn't watch it crash; I was already climbing the chain link ahead of me, going up and over just like I had when we were running from the carnies on the night of the wheel. I wasn't worried about the bike being stolen—it was three in the morning—so much as I wanted to get off the street and into the building on the other side of the fence. I'd ridden fast, faster than I ever had in my life, and I just might've left Tommy in the dust. If I had, then this whole thing would suddenly be a darn sight easier.

I couldn't see it from where I went over, but the sign mounted on the outside of the fence read THE FUTURE SITE OF FAIRMONT TOWERS, though me and the guys had pointed out to each other, time and again, that there was only the one tower. At ten stories it wasn't even much of a tower—not compared to some of the skyscrapers you'd find in Lafayette and other places—but it was still going to be the tallest building in Caina.

When they'd broken ground on the project back in the spring, we'd thought it would be something to see, this huge monolith twice as tall as the highest buildings around it. Then we'd realized, as the months went by, that putting up something that size would take time—lots and lots of time—and it quickly became just as boring as anything else in town. We'd kept track of it, though, waiting for some big development that would wow us. They'd slapped plywood around the lower eight floors like some rough skin growing up from the ground, but the top two floors weren't quite as finished yet, naked girders reaching into the sky like the skeleton of some dinosaur bigger than anything you'd see in a museum.

There weren't any doors or windows yet, just big square holes in that plywood skin where they were going to be, and I raced up the steps and through the wide front entrance without looking back. Inside the ground floor there were wooden studs everywhere, the bones of walls to come standing in lines like some bizarre forest. I slowed for a second to wrestle the flashlight out of my pocket, then whipped around, shining the light this way and that, looking for the security guard, or whomever was...

There was nothing behind me but that empty doorway and the night outside, and as I realized that I felt Tommy arrive. I took an involuntary step sideways, feeling suddenly crowded, like my personal space had been invaded. I took a reflexive swing with the flashlight, backhanding as I stepped again—and my arm jerked back, just as reflexively, as my hand slapped through air as cold as any winter day, though I was still sweating from my ride in the late summer heat.

It was as close as I'd come to any real contact with him, and I took a third step, turned, and dashed through the growing apartment building. *He's getting closer!* I thought as I ran. *Stronger!* Was this what had driven Ray out into the street? I pushed that thought away as I sprinted between two rows of naked beams—along what I thought would be a corridor—shining the light all around, running for the corner and looking for—

There they were, visible through the gaps between the studs: stairs, running up to the second floor and down to whatever was below the ground floor. I chose up and started climbing. Behind me, hugging so close I could feel the slight chill in the metal of the handrail, Tommy followed. I swore I could almost hear his trademark wheeze, but he was keeping up now, something that couldn't be outrun or left behind. My lungs were on fire by the fourth floor, my legs by the fifth, but I didn't stop, *couldn't* stop, aware of him the whole time.

I was wobbling when I burst out onto the unfinished ninth floor. Dizzy from the run and disoriented by the lack of outside walls up here, I staggered sideways and nearly right out of the building into thin air as the handrail ended. I yelled as I stumbled, seeing nothing out there but empty space and the rooftops across the street, gray slabs in the moonlight, even the highest of them so far below me.

My collarbone slammed into one of the wooden studs running from floor to ceiling, waiting for them to add the plywood skin that was working its way up the outside of the building. The pain was shocking, but my arms jerked forward as my knees buckled, wrapping the two-by-four in a desperate hug. My head was actually outside, and I had a clear view of my flashlight spinning out into the night and then down, down—oh, God, so far *down*—to shatter against the packed earth more than eighty feet below.

I don't think this is a good idea, came a familiar, whining voice in my head, and though it might have been a memory, I couldn't be sure. I stared at the spot where the flashlight had gone out, its broken pieces hidden by the night shadows about the base of the building, and the world seesawed around me. I yanked back from the edge and whirled, rubber-limbed as any town drunk, looking about desperately. I was high, a lot higher than the top of the Ferris wheel, but we were on a building-sized platform with a nice, solid floor, and Tommy was still here. He wasn't crowding as close as he had downstairs, but he was still here. I felt a cool breeze coming from the stairs as he apparently chilled the air around him. *I don't think this is a good idea*, I thought—or heard—again, but it was too late. I'd seen what I was looking for.

The studs were in place for the outer walls, but the inner walls hadn't been started on this floor—maybe because the ceiling wasn't complete. Above me was nothing but the outer edge of the tenth floor, an eight-foot walkway all the way around the open inner space like a railless balcony, probably just someplace for the workmen to stand as they finished the framework up there. Without any kind of permanent floor, there was no way to have stairs up to it, but in the corner behind the open pit of the stairway was a ladder leading up to the tenth floor-to-be.

I staggered toward it, passing close enough to the mouth of the stairs that I caught Tommy's chill, my stair-side arm feeling like it had taken a quick dunk in a bucket of ice water. Somewhere inside there was a part of me screaming to listen to Tagalong, that this *wasn't* a good idea, that I should at least wait until my legs had recovered, 'til I could walk a straight line again, before trying to climb a ladder—especially when I looked through that ladder and saw nothing but open space and night sky.

But if I stopped, if I gave myself time to think about what I was doing, then I might not be able to do it. I had to keep bulling ahead, because to stop was to let Tommy win again, and the deal would remain unbroken; Tommy would come with me to jail, where he'd have all the access to me he could want.

I'd be insane in a week. Maybe less.

So, I climbed the ladder as fast as I could, focusing my eyes on my destination instead of the rooftops of downtown below me in the distance. I didn't listen to the warning voice in my head, or the smashing of my heart against my ribs, or the rasp of my panicked breathing in my throat, so thick and loud I might've been mistaken for Wheezy Taglioni himself. The top of the ladder stuck far up above the edge of the walkway, allowing me to climb high enough to just step off sideways.

Without stopping I turned, grabbed the ladder and started pulling; I didn't know if he'd need a ladder, but I couldn't think what else to do. Just like always, he'd started following and we'd—I'd—started running, trying to stop him from catching up any way I knew how. It was an aluminum ladder, instead of heavy wood, and though for a terrifying moment I almost overbalanced and dove headfirst to level nine's plywood floor ten feet below, I caught myself and kept going. Hand-over-hand, rung-over-rung—rungs which grew cool, and then cold, the closer to the bottom of the ladder they were—I lifted the ladder up there with me, though small white starbursts started going off at the edges of my vision, looking way too much like the fireworks at the end of my dream for comfort. I pictured Tagalong standing on the floor below, looking up at me as he always looked at us when we fled his approach, shifting from foot-to-foot and saying—

"C'mon, wait up!"

The voice sent me reeling backward—that hadn't been in my head, I'd *heard* it! I rocked back, for the first time since scrambling up on the walkway completely aware of the lack of walls and the hundred-foot drop behind me. I sagged, started to fall—and was brought up short with a jolt as the top of the ladder crashed into the steel crossbeam above me with a thin, ringing clank. The foot of the ladder was still eighteen inches below the edge of the floor I was standing on, but the top rung was at least a foot above the girder that would eventually form the roof-edge. The shock had almost pulled the frigid aluminum from my fingers, and I hung there a moment, feet forward, butt back, my grip on the rungs still the only thing keeping me from tumbling backward and right out of the building. I took a breath, and then another.

"No fair!" came the familiar whine, and all of my skin felt like it was crawling. *"Wait up!"*

I pulled my weight back over my feet again, braced myself, yanked the ladder up and let it crash down to stand on the balcony with me, no longer providing a way up from the floor below.

"Wait up!"

"Go home, Tagalong," I shouted, hanging onto the ladder for balance as the starbursts in the corners of my vision grew and the floor swayed for me again. "Just go home! Please!" I paused, listening for more whining, but mostly just to catch the breath I'd started to lose back when I was climbing past the fourth floor—or was it the third? I gasped for air, listened, gasped again, and felt my face break into a smile at the silence coming from below. *It's working*, I thought. *I'm leaving him behind!*

And then the cold came pouring over the edge of the walkway, pouring up, over my feet, then my ankles, then rising to my shins.

"Wait up!"

The voice came from thin air just below me, and with it came a wave of that moist, mucus-breath stink, drifting over my face like an invisible mist, forcing its way into my mouth and nose. Again, the only thing that kept me from stumbling back and right out into the night was my grip on the ladder. I looked wildly left and right for somewhere else to go—anywhere else to go—but there was nowhere but this wide catwalk, and nothing up there with me, nothing but...

The ladder.

I swung around to the front of the ladder and started climbing, pushing away any thoughts that came my way. The steel girder was ten or twelve feet above the catwalk floor, and I kept my eyes on it the whole time, willing myself not to look down, or think about just how high I was, but I couldn't shake the image of that falling flashlight spinning into oblivion. *Just me and the ladder*, I thought. *There's nothing else but me and the ladder.*

I got to the steel I-beam hanging there in the night sky and managed to throw a leg over it. *It's like the monkey bars at the park*, I thought. *It's just like the monkey bars.*

"No fair! Wait up!"

He was still there, but fainter now, less demanding than before. I remembered how quiet he'd gotten while he'd stared at the Ferris wheel that day at the carnival, and how silent he'd been on the night of the ride. *He might be dead*, I thought, *but he's still afraid.*

Then the cold began working its way up my dangling legs. He was coming.

I knew he didn't need it, but I didn't know what else to do: I leaned forward and shoved the top of the ladder with all my strength. It slid away from me, hung in place for an instant, then overbalanced and continued to slide, falling sideways. It dipped below the edge of the girder, then fell forward and through the space where they had yet to put even the wooden studs. It fell flat, flipped up, and its own weight pulled it out of the tower to fly, end-over-end, toward that shattered flashlight.

The chill paused, then slowly began to rise again, enveloping me in a zone of winter, the summer sweat on my skin nearly crackling with the cold. That meaty moist stink assaulted my nose again—*grave breath*, I thought—and I knew he was near, close enough to touch, and I more than half expected to feel his icy dead palm come to rest on my shoulder.

He wasn't going to stop, I realized. He'd never stop. He couldn't. I suddenly recalled him standing at the carnival gate, convincing himself we'd just forgotten him. His forearm shook beneath my hand again as I told him he'd be okay and helped him onto the Ferris wheel that had so terrified him. Remembered tears warmed my chest, and I heard Mrs. Taglioni saying, *I can't tell you how many nights he sat at the dinner table telling me about you, Ray, and Jerry, and the way you all took care of him.* This was a kid who'd pretended we were friends so hard he'd fooled his own mother. He'd fooled himself. He'd *died* to have friends.

And... and we were welching on the deal.

It hit me with sudden clarity—I'd had parts of the problem racing through my head since I'd figured out what was happening, but I'd been too busy running to catch it, to really think the whole thing through. Tommy'd been terrified, but he'd also been a stand-up guy, right to the end, even though it had killed him. And what did *we* do, just as soon as he showed up looking for us to make good on our end? We ran, just the way we said we wouldn't. Ray got angry about it at first, and Jerry tried to weasel his way out at first, but in the end we all ran so far and so fast we were killing ourselves, as cowardly as Tommy'd been honorable. He wouldn't stop following until we stopped running. He couldn't.

This was Tommy Tagli-lonely.

"I'm sorry, Tommy," I burst out, words I'd thought in the past but never spoken. "I told you you'd be okay. We didn't think you'd get hurt. I'm so sorry. But you won, okay? You won and a deal's a deal. You're one of the gang now. But we can't hang out, man. You're dead. I can be your friend, but you're dead!"

The world swayed as a wave of dizziness swept over me, but whether it was left over from hauling ass up eight flights of stairs or because now my heart was racing out of control with terror, I had no idea. The why of it didn't really matter, though, as I threw myself full-length on the girder, clinging for dear life. It wasn't one of those huge I-beams I'd seen in pictures, a dozen hard-hatted workmen taking lunch along a girder two feet wide during the construction of the Empire State Building; this was narrower than my chest, oddly shaped, and slick with the sudden cold. The fingers of my left hand gripped the lower edge on the inside, but my legs, still rubbery from the long run up the building, were all but useless, the edges of the beam digging painfully into my thighs as they tried to squeeze the steel. The girder seemed to roll beneath me, the edge digging harder into my left inner thigh. With a shout I realized it wasn't the steel that was rolling, but me, slipping sideways as my fingers, under the beam and closest to Tommy—maybe even *in* him—went numb with the cold.

"You're one of the gang, now, right?" I shouted. "So we're friends! But I can't be your friend if I'm dead, too! I can't be your friend if I'm dead!"

I was still sliding, my weight pulling me out, around the beam and down. My right hand, sweat-slick and freezing, scrabbled at the bottom of the icy girder, searching desperately for something to grab, to hold, to help my slipping left hand stop me from—

My fingers lost the beam and I fell away, the world spinning about me in earnest as I screamed, nonstop, until the impact.

CHAPTER 16

IN A ROOM ALL ALONE

I opened my eyes to a world of soft white clouds.

It took a moment for everything to come into sharper focus, the ripples and whorls I first took for fluffy, edgeless clouds turning into the weird, irregular surface of acoustical ceiling tiles. Something beeped, and I blinked as it beeped again.

Then again.

Though I recognized the bleating heart monitor thingy from watching *General Hospital* with Mom, the rest of the stuff in the hospital room was a mystery to me. But I was in a hospital, no doubt about it. The air smelled like rubbing alcohol and Pine-Sol, and the bed was weirdly comfortable and uncomfortable at the same time. It was dark outside, so the room's bright fluorescent lights turned the wide window into a mirror.

I was thirsty, and it hit me that I'd been awake and looking around the room for over a minute now and I hadn't seen a nurse or doctor. There wasn't even any of that PA system noise that was always in the background whenever they showed a hospital on television. I started looking around for a call button or something. There had to be some way for me to call the nurse, or a doctor, right? I mean, they wouldn't just leave a kid in a room all alone, with no way to—

Wait. Back that up. Alone. I was... alone?

I waited. I listened. For want of a better word, I *felt*. I closed my eyes and imagined the sensation of Tommy Taglioni watching me, remembered the back of my neck crawling, the almost-tickle of breath against my ear and cheek, the odd, nameless sense that someone was inside my personal space.

Nothing. I was actually alone.

"It worked," I whispered, and, dry throat or not, I started laughing. The laugh cut itself short, however, when the door opened and a familiar face poked through.

"Hi there," it said. "Remember me?"

"Detective Howard," I said.

He broke into a broad smile. "Very good. Twenty minutes ago, you didn't have a clue who I was, and went right back to sleep. You gonna be with us for a while, you think?"

I nodded.

"Good. I have some questions for you, if you feel up to it."

I nodded again, and the detective's head disappeared. The door started to swing shut, then popped open wide as a man in a white coat bustled through. He looked really young—way younger than my regular doctor—but his name tag read DR. WELLING. Dr. Welling shone a penlight in my eyes and had me roll my head around while he felt my neck. Behind him stood Detective Howard, and I saw now he had one arm in a sling. I jerked my chin toward it after the doctor took the thermometer from under my tongue.

"What happened to you?"

"He," said Dr. Welling, fitting the stethoscope into his ears, "dislocated his arm saving your life. You might want to thank him for that, young man."

The doctor bustled out, and the detective pulled up a chair. "There's an officer letting your parents know where you are right about now—we've been here less than an hour, so he might have to wake them up. Then they'll have to get here, so it'll be a little while yet. You being a minor, you don't have to talk to me until they get here, if you don't want to. How's about I tell you what I know while we wait?"

That sounded okay, so he got started. Something was going on, he said, something with the kids on my street. They were dropping like flies, and no one could figure out why. Three kids in the space of a week, with only one left—well, you didn't need to be a detective to know he'd have to keep an eye on me. "Your mom didn't want me to talk to you yet," he said. "But that didn't mean I had to leave you entirely alone."

So, he'd stationed some police around the neighborhood to keep an eye on our house, trying to keep me safe. "And to see if you went anywhere," he admitted. "Two of the other boys slipped out of the house in the night and never made it back. We wanted to keep an eye on you."

It turned out that my instincts had been good, and they had been watching me from Mrs. Boardman's—but from inside the house, not her yard. I sort of tuned Howard out for a minute then. So that was what I'd felt in my room; I'd been being watched by a bunch of cops with flesh-and-blood eyeballs, not some kid back from the dead. And in other parts of the house... well, weren't Mom and Dad keeping an eye on me?

"When your light went on in the middle of the night," Howard said, "the officers on watch called me in. I was just pulling into your neighborhood when you came out of the driveway and started heading toward Main. There was a whole team waiting to follow you, but any kind of motion would've been suspicious at the time of night, so once you were on Main they all pulled back, and it was just me."

So I *had* been being followed on my ride. My stomach churned: I mean, it was kind of good to find a rational explanation for so much, but... I'd gotten an hour of rest, with no dreams, and I felt a little more clearheaded than I had in what seemed like days, and right there and then, in that bright room that was all about sense and order, the idea of a fat, four-eyed ghost chasing me through the Caina night seemed just a little ridiculous. Mom had been worried about how everything was affecting me, and Jerry'd always said I was gullible. Was it all stress? Emotional exhaustion? Hallucinations? Had I just been trying to outrun my guilt? Jerry had thought Ray was crazy, and I'd wondered if Jerry was; what if we'd been right? I kind of understood now, Jerry saying he might have preferred crazy, because crazy can be cured, but the thought that I might have actually been losing my mind... I wasn't exactly sure how I felt about that.

"You almost lost me when you went over the fence— I didn't see your bike in the bushes, started to go right by— but when I saw the flashlight working its way around inside the Fairmont, I headed in. I got to the eighth floor and heard you yelling, but I'd lost the visual. I'd just realized you were up on the unfinished floors when that damn ladder fell by—scared the hell out of me, but at least I knew where you were."

He'd run to where the ladder had gone past, intending to lean out the window-hole and see if he could spot my flashlight that way—and I'd just been falling by, screaming and flailing. He'd managed to grab my ankle as I went past, turning my fall into a hard swing against the building's plywood wall, knocking me out and dislocating his shoulder.

"I might not have been able to pull you in if the rest of the officers hadn't arrived right then. But they did. And here we are."

Mom and Dad burst in then, and things got loud. Mom cried, and Dad shouted at me for worrying my mother like this, but they both hugged me. They turned on Detective Howard then, wanting him to leave me alone, but the officer who fetched them must've told them about Howard's snagging me out of the air, and the very prominent sling took some of the wind out of their sails.

"I have questions," Howard said, raising his voice a little. "And they need answers. You can stay—you can sit right there," he indicated two chairs, "but I'm asking."

"It's okay," I said, as my parents looked at me with huge eyes. I nodded. They sat.

"All right, then," said Howard, turning to me. "Let's start with something easy, okay?"

I nodded again.

"Who was your friend in the Fairmont?"

I closed my eyes. I'd forgotten I was shouting at my hallucination—of course Howard would have heard it.

"I—" I started, but stopped, unsure of where to start. I mean, how do you admit to someone that you've gone a little crazy? Maybe even more than a little.

"There was someone else there?" my father said. "There was someone else there and you let him get away?" He looked at me. "This other person—who was it? Did he push you? Is that why you—"

"No," I said, eyes still closed. I wasn't sure how I'd tell them this. "No, it was... I..."

"You were arguing," said Howard. "He was telling you something wasn't fair, and to wait, but you were telling him to go home. Then he... what?"

My eyes had opened very wide, and I stared at the detective. "You... you *heard* him?"

"I heard him shouting, and one of the responding officers heard him running down the stairwell as we were pulling you back into the building. He gave chase, but lost him in the dark. We know he was there, so who was he?"

"But... you heard him? Going away?"

Going away—just what we'd always asked him to do. And it didn't feel like he'd come back. He might've assumed I was dead—that he'd seen me fall and thought it was over with—but I didn't think so. I thought he'd finally gotten what he'd always wanted himself: he was one of the gang. He'd died trying to get that, and maybe if either Ray or Jerry'd said it to him, admitted he'd won and was one of us, they'd still be alive.

If we'd just told him that before the carnival, just treated him better, even Tommy'd still be alive.

Howard was growing annoyed with my questions. "Yes, we heard him. You know something—we know you do, son—and it'll only help you now to tell us." He leaned in closer, voice hardening. "Three boys are dead, and you were almost number four. There's someone else involved in whatever's going on, and I want to know his name. I want to know his name, and I want to know what's going on, and I want to know now."

Jerry's reform school speech rose up in my head, but there was nothing I could do about that now—there hadn't been for a while, not since Jerry went missing—and I didn't have Jerry and Ray to worry about anymore. Just me. It occurred to me, and not for the first time, that if we'd gone to the police right at the beginning of all this, my two best friends might still be alive. Even Mrs. Taglioni, and her never-ending tears; she'd hate me for sure—hate all of us— but maybe knowing what had happened would help in some way. The guilt—and the possibility of getting out from under some of it—mixed with the strange relief I felt that I might just not be crazy had me almost giddy, even in the presence of police and parents.

Besides, Tommy Tagalong had ridden the wheel, and won the deal. He might be dead, but he was one of us now; I might as well start acting like it.

"I... I'll tell you everything I know. It'll sound crazy, but there's nothing I can do about that. I think I have to tell it from the beginning, okay?"

Howard nodded. I looked at my parents, who stared back. "It's kind of a long story," I warned. My mother took my father's hand, and he nodded for the both of them. I looked at Detective Howard. "Everything would've..."

I turned to Mom and Dad, and tears came to my eyes.

"I'm so sorry."

I turned back to the detective and took a breath.

"Everything would've been different if we hadn't been such incredible assholes..."

BEHIND THE STORY

Where do you get your ideas?

The question, one every writer hears eventually (it's neat at first, like rite of passage, but quickly palls) is kind of a nightmare for me. At this point in time I write more short stories than anything else (this is my longest published work to date), and I honestly get ideas from everywhere: commercials, things people say and do, other people's writing (and I read constantly), and out of the great nebulous whatsis where stories just sit around waiting to be born. Often, by the time anyone asks about a particular story, I have no recollection where it came from, and simply claim it was from the great nebulous whatsis. In my case, I refer to that whatsis as the Great Mulch Pile of the Mind: a space in my head where shit just gets thrown and not thought about, all the bits, both useful and useless, where they break down and warm up and occasionally something sprouts, feeding on all the other stuff in that part of the pile. Often it's a weed, but sometimes it's a flower, and I try to nurture and care for and cultivate it until it's ready for me to pluck and share.

This one, however, I do remember: as so many of the better ones do, it grew from a variety of sources coming together to make a whole that's greater than the sum of its parts.

I belong to The Storyside, a collaborative of (at the time of this writing) five authors all dedicated to professionalism and quality. Every eighteen months or so, we put out an anthology of our work, which, at the moment, is a dark fiction series titled Insanity Tales. The particular volume we were writing in 2016 was subtitled *Seasons of Shadow*, so I needed a seasonal story, and I somewhat randomly chose summer.

Summer, I thought. *Kids. Summer vacation. No more classrooms, no more books, no more teachers' dirty looks.*

To be fair, I had just read my first Richard Laymon novel (yes, I know, I was late to the party as far as Laymon is concerned), *The Traveling Vampire Show*, and loved it. *Vampire Show* is about a group of kids in summer, and I can't swear this wasn't in my mental mulch pile and feeding this idea. That possibility is strengthened when you remember (if you've read *Vampire Show*) that Laymon's kids are trying to go to a traveling show set up just outside of town. Sound familiar?

I didn't have a vampire in mind, however. Even before summer and kids, I'd thought of what I wanted to base my story around: laundry.

Well, not laundry per se, but the feeling I get when I *do* my laundry. The washer and dryer are in the basement, you understand, and I'm usually using them in the middle of the night. Whether I've just put the stuff in the washer, transferred it to the dryer, or am carrying the basket full of warm, sweet-smelling shirts and pants upstairs for folding, there comes a time when I've turned off the basement lights and am climbing back up to the kitchen, the only illumination the bare and yellowed (why are they always yellowed?) bulb at the top of the stairs. It's during this walk up from the dark and hidden space beneath the house that the feeling strikes—not every time, but often enough.

There's something behind me.

I know there's nothing really there, but for that trip up from the dark there's a part of me that knows, is positive, that something is, and it's getting closer, sometimes maybe even about to touch me. I never look. You can't in these situations, can you? Because as long as you haven't seen anything, that part of your mind that knows there's nothing there has an edge; it can be logical and sensible, and all *in-*

chargey, and tamp down the part of your mind telling you to run, run now, get the fuck out of there! If you turn back, you're telling that little niggling feeling you think there may be something there, weakening the position of your logical mind. And besides... what if it's actually right?

It's childish, I'll admit... but I'll bet you know what I'm talking about. You've felt it—I think we all have—walking into a room alone, or strolling along a quiet street, that there is someone behind you, or beside you, but when you look, of course, there's no one. We pass it off as nerves, or déjà vu, or our subconscious playing tricks on us, or a multitude of other things, and we're probably right.

Probably.

I wanted to play with the idea of that feeling, and this was my chance. Since I like ghost stories (they're the most versatile members of the Things That Go Bump in the Night club, I think), it was the most natural (supernatural?) thing in the world to turn that feeing into a haunting.

So, there were all the basic elements of the story: kids on summer vacation, the spooky feeling that something is behind you, and someplace for those kids to try to escape that feeling (the Ferris wheel). I sat down and got to work meeting the kids, letting them tell me the story of Wheezy Taglioni and the circumstances surrounding his death. A couple of weeks later, as the story cruised past the 20,000-word mark and I realized it was nowhere near the end, I remembered this was supposed to be for a short story anthology.

Whoops!

But by that time, I was just too in love with the kids to stop, and too enamored of the story to try to simple it down. If you've ever read *Insanity Tales III: Seasons of Shadow*, you know I went back and wrote two completely different stories for it—then got to work trying to get *Friends in High Places* into shape to flog around to publishers.

So there, I've told you how it started, and you're holding the finished product in your hands. I guess only one question remains:

How'd I do?

—Rob Smales
9/5/2018

ABOUT THE AUTHOR

Rob Smales is the author of *Echoes of Darkness,* which garnered both a five-star Cemetery Dance Online review and a 2016 Pushcart nomination. With over two dozen short stories published, his story "Photo Finish" was also nominated for a Pushcart Prize and won the Preditors & Editors' Readers Choice Award for Best Horror Short Story of 2012. His story "A Night at the Show" received honorable mention on Ellen Datlow's list of the *Best Horror of 2014,* while "Death of the Boy" and "In Full Measure" made the same honorable mentions list for 2016. Most recently, he edited the dark humor anthology *A Sharp Stick in the Eye (and other funny stories)* for Books & Boos Press.

ALSO FROM
BLOODSHOT BOOKS

When Adam was 15, a terrible thing happened. So terrible that he and his father ran away in an attempt to put it behind them. But the past is not so easy to shake off. And a new start does not necessarily mean a better start. Who is the figure at the top of the stairs? Whose is the face in the mirror? What is the thing in the pond? And why does Adam often feel he is being followed, only for his pursuers to dissolve into shadow when he turns to confront them?

When Adam was 15, a terrible thing happened. So terrible that he believed it to be the worst thing of all. But he is about to find out that there are far worse things waiting out there....

Available in paperback or Kindle on Amazon.com

From a crater lake on an island off the coast of Bronze Age Estonia...

To a crippled Viking warrior's conquest of England ...

To the bloody temple of an Aztec god of death and resurrection...

Their presence has shaped our world. They are the Riders.

One month ago, an urban explorer was drawn to an abandoned asylum in the mountains of northern Massachusetts. There he discovered a large specimen jar, containing something organic, unnatural and possibly alive.

Now, he and a group of unsuspecting individuals have discovered one of history's most horrific secrets. Whether they want to or not, they are caught in the middle of a millennia-old war and the latest battle is about to begin.

Available in paperback or Kindle on Amazon.com
http://amzn.to/1peMAjz

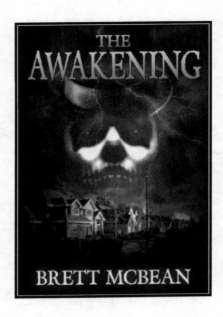

Welcome to the small Midwestern town of Belford, Ohio. It's summer vacation and fourteen-year-old Toby Fairchild is looking forward to spending a lazy, carefree summer playing basketball, staying up late watching monster movies, and camping out in his backyard with his best friend, Frankie.

But then tragedy strikes. And out of this tragedy an unlikely friendship develops between Toby and the local bogeyman, a strange old man across the street named Mr. Joseph. Over the course of a tumultuous summer, Toby will be faced with pain and death, the excitement of his first love, and the underlying racism of the townsfolk, all while learning about the value of freedom at the hands of a kind but cursed old man.

Every town has a dark side. And in Belford, the local bogeyman has a story to tell.

Available in paperback or Kindle on Amazon.com

http://bit.ly/AWAKEpb

ON THE HORIZON FROM
BLOODSHOT BOOKS

2018*

Killer Chronicles – Somer Canon
The Winter Tree – Mark Morris
The Special – James Newman & Mark Steensland
Victoria (What Hides Within #2) – Jason Parent

2019-20*

Bleed Away the Sky – Brian Fatah Steele
The Devil Virus – Chris DiLeo
The October Boys – Adam Millard
The Cryptids – Elana Gomel
What Sleeps Beneath – John Quick
Dead Branches – Benjamin Langley
Dead Sea Chronicles – Tim Curran
Blood Mother: A Novel of Terror – Pete Kahle
Not Your Average Monster – World Tour
The Abomination (The Riders Saga #2) – Pete Kahle
The Horsemen (The Riders Saga #3) – Pete Kahle

other titles to be added when confirmed

BLOODSHOT BOOKS

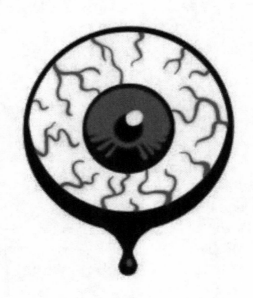

READ UNTIL YOU BLEED!

Made in the USA
Lexington, KY
28 September 2018